T0151756

SLUM

CHARCO PRESS

First published by Charco Press 2017

Charco Press Ltd., Office 59, 44-46 Morningside Road, Edinburgh EH10 4BF

Copyright © Gabriela Cabezón Cámara 2009
English translation copyright © Frances Riddle 2017

This book was originally published in Spanish under the title
La Virgen Cabeza in 2009 by Eterna Cadencia (Argentina).
The rights of Gabriela Cabezón Cámara to be identified as the author of
this work and of Frances Riddle to be identified as the translator of this
work have been asserted by them in accordance with the Copyright, Designs
and Patents Act 1988.

ISBN: 978 1 9997227 0 8
e-book: 978 1 9997227 1 5

www.charcopress.com

Edited by Annie McDermott
Cover design by Pablo Font
Typeset by Laura Jones
Proofread by Ellen Jones

2   4   6   8   10   9   7   5   3

Gabriela Cabezón Cámara

SLUM VIRGIN

Translated by Frances Riddle

CHARCO PRESS

CONTENTS

AUTHOR'S NOTE

In the neighbourhood I grew up in people were poor but not terribly poor. No one was wealthy. They bought their homes with loans, they were housewives, mechanics, salesmen, plumbers. And they knew that we – their children – who played catch and football together in the streets, and climbed trees and threw ourselves onto the piles of sand from the first floors of the two-story houses that at some point they started to build on the empty lots around the corner, they knew that our quality of life would be better than theirs because theirs was better than their parents'. And perhaps their parents had had a better standard of living that their grandparents, but I can't know that for sure because the proletariat does not keep family trees.

I had grandparents. With them, one day, I discovered the world of flowers: it happened in my grandfather's small front garden, which was also my grandmother's. But the flowers weren't hers, or theirs, the flowers were his. As were the hens and the vegetable plot and the fig tree, pomegranate tree and – I think – the other flowers I got to see another day, some tiny, purple flowers that grew wildly on their own, without the need for anyone to do anything, not even my grandfather. But the day I discovered flowers, they were white and there were a lot of them and they had bloomed suddenly, all white and very many of them, on the bare branches of a tree which – up until the time before (what time was that?) – had not shown a single leaf. In front of my parents' house there is – still – a small garden and to the side, a kind of patio with big red paving stones that in summer, once the sun has set, retains the afternoon warmth. There, on the still-hot stones, beside the geraniums and very near the ash trees, or sometimes on the grass that my mother defended from stray dogs, I learned to study the night sky. The full moon would emerge from the edge of the bus stop, six blocks to the north, hand in hand with a very bright star. Venus, I believe. The huge golden moon would become whiter as the hours went by. I grew up convinced that the valleys of the moon were the Three Wise Men. I could see their crowns. Watching the stars was something I learned to do in tandem with other luminaria: fireflies that floated in the air weaving a tapestry of tiny lights that moved up and down, generating a sparkling density. Once I caught some and put them in a jar, the 'fireflies jar'. Poor things.

My dad arrived home from work at 9 p.m. For forty years, every day. In December, once school had broken up for summer and we could go to bed later, we'd wait for my father there, in the front yard. He'd come from the north, like the moon; except he came from the bus stop on a journey that included a bus, a subway and a train. Back then my understanding of geography went as far as the centre (the place where my dad worked), my neighbourhood, my grandparents' neighbourhood not far from mine, and Mar del Plata. It must have been in this way that I acquired a notion of the periphery.

My periphery was a peaceful one, that is if we don't take into account the intra-family clashes. No, no, they don't count. Once there was a thief, a thief! A thief! Shouted the next-door neighbour and we couldn't help but hear her, because the houses bought with loans, laboriously, shared their backyards. That's why we heard everyone's arguments and everyone heard ours, and we all ran out into the street together, the entire block, when the thief tried to escape over the roofs and the police showed up with their blue cars outside our doors. I am not sure he was a thief. The suburbs were peaceful and that was the only time the police came to the neighbourhood. But in the mornings, on Saturdays, when there was no school and Dad was at work, we would gather up spent bullet casings and line up like an army, if armies lined up from shortest to tallest like they lined us up at school. I'd make an effort to stay near the older kids and managed to succeed despite my short stature: in any case, I'd be at the end of the line and I felt tall all the same, because of the position I held. I should have known then that many things, most things, between people come down to a matter of position.

As I've said, my dad worked in the centre – as we used to call the busiest part of the city – and sometimes we'd go and visit. We walked six blocks, took a bus, walked another ten blocks, took a train and from there, from the train station, went down to take the subway. In summer, Dad worked in Mar del Plata. Then we got to do the only thing my mother ever wanted to do: go and spend time with her mother and sisters who all lived there. I loved it because my mom was happy and relaxed and hardly disciplined us. Except in extraordinary circumstances, like the time she sent me to run errands, to get some bread and eggs, and I had the brilliant idea to play with the bag: I put it on the ground, kicked it lightly so that the bag would jump a little and so on and so forth. All the way home, an entire block. The eggs did not make it whole.

Back then, save for the family disputes, it was a peaceful life. We didn't quite understand what the spent casings were, and when we learned about the bullets, we were certain that they'd belonged to the Lone Ranger. For us, wealthy folk were the likes of Donald Duck's rich uncle and poor people were the Biafra kids, who were super skinny and had huge bellies. In Religion class they told us that we had to be good to the poor and we'd daydream about travelling and being missionaries and saving African children.

Until I turned thirteen. Then a war broke out and the dictatorship came to an end and I learned that people had disappeared and that there were torture centres more or less near my home. I also saw a photo. It was taken in San Isidro, a neighbourhood near mine, where my high school was. A line divided the image in two. It was a wall. On one side were five mansions with very lush gardens and vast swimming pools. On the other, dozens of very tiny rudimentary shacks all jumbled together, with tin roofs held in place with only the weight of the stones sitting on them. Also around that time I realised that I fancied a classmate, a girl, and I wanted to kiss her. The world exploded around me. The family fallouts increased, I began to wander alone in the centre looking for friends. I made friends with a transvestite, who I loved. I loved her sense of humour and I was scared of the police who were always hounding her and her friends who were all minors and who, to avoid being put in jail, let the police rape them. I learned about poverty in the closest possible way. I experienced the cruelty of the streets and also discovered an ability to laugh in any circumstance. All this thanks to my dear friend and her friends. Then, life happened, in a rush like a mudslide, and here I am. Writing this author's note and trying to explain *Slum Virgin* for readers in a faraway land that has its own poverty, homelessness, wealth, religions. A world that's very different but also similar because we are not that far apart.

And we all experience love and pain and struggles and faith, and laughter and death with the intensity offered by the lives we build. To you, dear reader, *¡salud!*

Gabriela Cabezón Cámara
Abasto, Buenos Aires
January 2020

For Ana, my love
For Karina, Lola, Lautaro and Amparo

1. QUITY: 'EVERYTHING THAT'S BORN HAS TO DIE'

Atoms, molecules whipped into a frenzy by random chance, that's all life is. This was the kind of profound insight that filled my head out there on the island in the Delta, half-naked and without any of my things, not even a computer, just a little bit of cash and the credit cards I couldn't use until we left Argentina. My thoughts were rotten: sticks, beer bottles, lily pads, used condoms, crumbling docks and headless dolls, a collage of losses discarded by the tide. I felt like a castaway who'd barely survived a shipwreck. Although I've learnt by now that no one ever really survives a shipwreck. The ones who drown end up dead and the ones who are saved spend the rest of their lives drowning.

We stayed in the town of Tigre on the Paraná Delta the whole winter, engulfed by the fog from the river that flowed endlessly past. We didn't speak much. For me, everything was underscored by pain, suffused with it. I floated through daily life, alien to everything that sustained me: the smells of the kitchen and the heat of the wood-burning stove. Cleopatra exercised all her talents under the shadow of the Virgin, ignoring my dazed indifference to life and death, to the whims of deranged molecules that lay waste to worlds and children in the course of their adventures. I lived folded in on myself in the foetal position, just like the creature growing inside of me and in spite of me: my womb was alive with a daughter who continued to grow even though I was a cemetery of dead loved ones. I felt like a stone: an aberration, a state of matter, a rock imbued with the knowledge that it was going to be crushed and reconfigured and transformed into something else. And this knowledge hurt. I haven't done any scientific research on the topic, but surely you never get two rocks that are exactly alike. Or maybe you do – who the hell could ever compare all the rocks of all time? And I don't know that it would lessen the pain for this rock to know that maybe, once, there had been another identical rock somewhere in the expanses of time, one that doesn't even exist any more. All that exists are the movements of molecules, the fundamental restlessness of the elements. I don't give a fuck whether there's ever been or never been another aberration identical to me or to Kevin. Nature doesn't conform to the rules of mass production: 'It's not an assembly line, the products aren't all the same, because there's God,' said Cleopatra. 'There is no God,' I told her sometimes, the few times I ever spoke, when she came in with the analgesic of her exuberant and optimistic imagi-nation. Little stories about Kevin in a paradise of PlayStations with huge screens – 'Just picture it, Quity, the screen is the world, my love' – and the Virgin Mary as Mum and God as Grandpa. Because Cleo had the familial complexities of the Holy Trinity all worked out; according to her, God would be the Virgin's father. 'So he's Jesus's father too, Cleo?' I asked. 'Wouldn't that be like incest?' 'Oh, darling, you mean incest like that cockroach Carlos who fucked his daughter and left her pregnant and we gave him the beating of a lifetime but the child was already properly screwed up and properly pregnant anyway?' 'Yes, Cleo, incest, or like you say: he's a cockroach.' 'Look, Quity, how could God be anything like that piece of shit Paraguayan, stop fucking around. Jesus is the son of Mary alone.' Firm in her theological certainties and her genealogical connections, she continued with her part of the dialogue that we repeated almost every day on the island: 'I'm coming from a place of love, Quity, I want you to know where Kevin is. He's in heaven, you idiot. He's happy.' 'Sure, Cleo, and he's eating ambrosia cookies, right?'

Death pained me. His and mine and my daughter's, even though she wasn't alive yet in the strict sense of the word, that is to say she still hadn't been born. Everything hurt. When your consciousness opens up to death or death opens up to your consciousness an abyss rips through the centre of your being, leaving cracks of lacerating emptiness, emptiness that anguishes, asphyxiates, obsesses, and all you can do is wait for it to pass.

I used to dream of the dead, of everyone who'd ever died, buried one on top of the other for centuries and millennia until they formed part of the earth's crust. But what tortured me most were the images of my own dead rapidly decaying thanks to the third-rate wood of their cheap coffins, making new dirt for the Boulogne Cemetery in Buenos Aires. Kevin, Jonas, Jessica, all of them had turned to dirt on me, to humus and the warm, wet plains of the Pampas, fertiliser for the carnations and geraniums that adorned their miserable tombs.

Thousands of years after Homer, when nothing was left of his world except a few shitty columns piled up for the entertainment of tourists and archaeologists, I dreamed of Kevin with the same desperation as Odysseus when he dreamed of his mother. It's still impossible to hug the dead, composed as they are only of memory, which also dies in the end.

I dreamt of Kevin. He could appear at any point in any dream and it would never be shocking: I'd be at home and I'd come across him, always in the morning and always in the

3

kitchen. I'd seen the footage of my little boy's body, distorted by death, blood flowing from his head until he dried up and then the blood dried up. But I'd find him in the kitchen in the morning and it didn't surprise me: I'd been hoping to see him and no one's very surprised when they encounter something they've been hoping for, even if they've been hoping against all realistic expectations. Almost out of reflex I'd give him some milk and his favourite biscuits, the ones shaped like animals. I picked out all the red elephants for him, for Kevin. My little boy, I thought.

His death had ended up shining a light on my maternity: it had made me his mother. And there, in the kitchen, in my dreams, he would tell me what he'd done on the days since we'd last seen each other. And nothing had happened. He told me about what life in the slum was like without me, as if it weren't he and the slum that were no longer there, but just me that was missing. I mean, as if they weren't all dead and him too, as if the slum hadn't been bulldozed over and converted into the cement guts of a real-estate venture, and he, Kevin, my boy, hadn't been converted into a little jumble of bones and worms squirming in the belly of a nearby plot of land, right there in the Boulogne Cemetery.

But the moment Kevin tried to grab the cup of milk the dream splintered and cut me, sending pain ripping through my body: he couldn't drink the milk or eat the biscuits that made his little black eyes sparkle as if those eyeballs were still filled with life. Not much time had passed but the eyeballs, I think, are the quickest to decay in bodies when they stop being bodies and become something else, as blindly and inexorably as lava turns into rock and a bunch of rocks into an island and then an island back into a bunch of pieces of rock. He was trying to grab the milk but he couldn't: his little hand passed through the cup, which by this point in the dream was as solid as anything else in the world and not about to let itself be picked up by a ghost. And then the death that tormented me most repeated itself, and nothing else mattered any more. I could hardly feel anything as I tried to sit him on my knee, as I tried and failed to help him drink his milk. But I felt something beating against my lap and it was so impossible that something could beat and not be alive that I couldn't help but try and hug him, as if death were merely a procedural error. I tried a thousand times without ever taking hold of anything but air, and I ended up hugging myself again and again, alone, accompanied only by the beating of a heart that wasn't mine. I would wake up crying, almost suffocating, and it was true: Kevin was no more, he was totally dead, turning to dirt in the cemetery. Who knows, I thought, through roots and photosynthesis he might end up somehow becoming air, water, a storm. What a load of crap – he could just as easily be a salad or an earthworm used as catfish bait and most likely he was nothing at all, nothing more than what I could remember of him.

What was beating was my tiny daughter and I held my belly with my hands to hug her. I'd often go back to sleep and dream of her: my daughter being born a fragile little baby like they all are, as wounded by death as anyone else, a passing whim of matter like everything else. But then my little girl used to turn into a little turtle and I could carry her in my pocket and if she fell out it was fine, she just stuck her feet and head inside her shell and lay there belly up, rocking on the curve of her back made of minerals until I reached down and put her back in my pocket.

It's always made me feel safer to carry the most important things right up against my body. That's where I carried my gun for years, and I still carry my money and a good luck charm close to my skin. But even though I carried her inside my body I didn't feel safe about María Cleopatra. I was afraid she'd be born dead, a little body already turning into something else, not even dirt but a clot of my blood, and whenever I felt her move I found a moment of peace, some sense of bearable order to the universe.

But then I'd fall asleep again. I never knew if it was the pregnancy or the weight of the recent deaths that made me sleep through most of the time we spent on the island while Cleo did I don't know what. Pretty much everything, I suppose. She was my mother and my father and my provider. She dressed me and fed me. She collected firewood and brought in a television and that's how we lived and that's how I survived during the few hours I spent awake. Because my life, I mean this being made up of matter that is me, is not without its spirit of perseverance, its will to continue being.

I spent months this way, sleeping, looking out of the window or listening to the sounds of the delta. I heard what I'd never heard before: the mud piling up among the reeds, the seeds bursting into roots, the tension of the trees holding the edges of the island together. And the water, the deep sounds of the rising and falling of the tide. And I heard what I couldn't possibly have heard: Kevin's little body bursting into putrid bubbles as the water fulfilled its desire to return to itself and leave the dust to dust.

2. QUITY: 'WE WERE GIVEN A NEW LIFE'

We were given a new life
by the American Dream
we took over Florida
making all our fans scream.

It took a long time, but the fog finally lifted. My daughter woke me up, all mine that morning like never before and like so few times after, stomping joyfully inside me. I began to feel like I too was floating in a warm bright fluid: the only shadows were the soft and restless shapes cast by the willow branches that combed the air between my window and the river.

'Good morning, Quity, my love!' Cleo was beginning to appear. Sweet and chatty as she is, she never appears out of nowhere: you always know she's coming. This morning she was all domesticity with *mate* and pastries, and I first heard her, then smelled her, and then finally saw her. She threw herself onto the bed and gave me a kiss, such a passionate one that her makeup smeared, one set of her fake eyelashes fell off and her Doris Day hairdo was ruined. 'The sleeping beauty has awoken!' she said, starting to laugh, her teeth shining. She's pure happiness, white and radiant and queer and devout and adoring and she speaks like she's constantly singing a bolero about a bride on her way to the altar. 'Come, my light, my love, my wife, the three of us are having lunch at Fondeadero because I got a canoe and you and I have a lot to talk about. You'll see, today's going to be an unforgettable day.'

On the way there, under the bright sunlight that reflected off the river, I could sense the cold hands of my dead, with their hairless knuckles and the pain that I couldn't stop imagining, the solitary agony of a five-year-old boy, tugging at me. I felt like a traitor for making the survivor's mistake of carrying on living. But I couldn't let go of his little dead hand. I promised I'd get revenge, knowing that as long as I was preparing the weapons I could keep him alive. I felt like I had a double pregnancy: a live daughter, growing but yet to have a face or a voice, and a dead son, with a face and a voice that were inexorably dissolving into nothingness.

That day I let myself be carried along by the happiness of being alive. Our little daughter was doing somersaults inside me like an astronaut in an antigravity chamber and I thought that was her vote in favour of life, of the green colours of the native flora on the opposite bank and the reds and ochres of the imported trees on our side of the Canal Honda. And the river: 'I was a river in the evening, / and the trees sighed inside me, / and the path and the grasses ended in me. / A river ran through me, a river ran through me!' I recited the verses of Juan L. for Cleopatra and she started to speak: 'That's pretty, Quity, but don't start doing evening things when it's not even noon yet. You have to understand, my love, that they're in heaven and we're on earth. I know you don't believe in heaven, even though you're wrong because it's real, but what you can't argue about is that we're on earth. And if there's a heaven, like I know there is, you can be happy. And if not, there's even more reason to celebrate: we have to make the most of this short while we're alive. Feel it, Quity, feel the sun. And also, darling, we're going to be mothers.' 'So what, Cleo?' I was finally able to get a word in. 'Now we're entitled to tell the rest of humanity to fuck off?' Cleopatra sighed: 'No, Quity, you don't have to tell anyone to fuck off, but our daughter has the right to be happy and our duty is to take care of her above all else. And yes, we can be selfish like every other mother in the world, even the Virgin says so: if it had been up to her, Jesus would've been a carpenter and married to Mary Magdalene. Even if she was a whore, it was better than being a messiah and marrying a cross. Because it's better for children to live, whether or not they come back to life when they die.' 'I'm with you on that, Cleo,' I said, laughing. But Cleopatra didn't stop there. 'The Virgin says that being alive is the best, and Achilles knew as much when he was in Hades. When that guy who took ten years to get home – what was his name? Ulysseem? When he said to him "Oh, hello, king of the dead," Achilles answered: "Give me a break, Ulysseem: I'd rather be a slave or an indigent" – an indigent is like a poor person, Quity – "and be alive than reign over the kingdom of the dead."'

My daughter enjoyed the speeches of the queerer of her two mothers, seeming to dance as we listened to her. As for me, they threw me into confusion. How could she cite *The Odyssey* almost word for word? She'd never read it in her fucking life. Where the hell did she get things like that from? Maybe the Virgin actually did exist and was into the classics as well as poor prostitutes.

'Look, Cleo, your daughter's moving.' Cleo dropped her half-eaten *empanada* and prophetic tone and rubbed my belly: 'Hello, princess, I'm your other mum, Cleopatra, the one who feeds the two of you, the one who's knitting your little clothes. We're going to leave this place, my baby.' Cleo turned serious and resumed her prophesying: 'We're going to another country. You're going to be born there, it's a place with a lot of sun, palm trees, a green sea. The only bad part, the Virgin Saint told me, Quity, is that it's full of *gusanos*.' 'Oh no, darling,' I said firmly, 'you can go ahead and tell your Virgin that there's no way in hell I'm going to Cuba.' 'Quity, I said *gusanos*, not *cubanos*.' 'And don't they all come from Cuba, darling?' 'Yes, but the *gusanos* are the ones that leave, Quity. Don't play dumb.'

And here we are, in Miami, surrounded by *gusanos*, or worms, as if all of us who lived in the slum were condemned more or less to the same fate. Of course, these worms aren't quite the same as the ones in the Boulogne Cemetery: the worms here in Miami are human, mostly claim to miss Cuba constantly, have lots of money and work like crazy. Most Cubans in Miami live off government subsidies in exchange for being evidence of the evils of Socialist revolutions, and all they do is get drunk, take drugs and beat their wives. Even so, you often see their wives on Eighth Street in the mornings, looking for their husbands in the dive bars where they fall like trees. After the seventh drink, the rum hits them like an axe. They begin to lose their height and balance, they run into someone, slur, stammer out a string of curses, wobble for an instant, then hit the ground and it's over, they stay there until someone picks them up. Helena used to have to go from dive bar to dive bar as well until Torito died, but Torito wasn't a worm and he didn't hit Helena. They were the only other ones who followed the same route as Cleo and me: slum – massacre – Miami.

The worms follow Cleo everywhere, her and the head of the Virgin, that poor homage to the poor that's now considered a relic. That chunk of painted cement that also survived the massacre and that Cleo lugged across America and all the way up the social ladder until we got to Miami and began to open our numerous bank accounts.

But the road was long. That bright morning on the island when we began to think only about the three of us, we went for lunch at Fondeadero dressed in what little we had. Cleo wore the clothes of the lady who owned the house, the TV talk show host diva who'd taken Cleo under her wing and given her the keys to her mansion in Tigre so she could go whenever she wanted. I put on some men's clothes, who knows who they belonged to but they were the only things that fit me at that point in the pregnancy, which wasn't so very far along but I was already showing. Cleo's six-foot-two frame managed to squeeze into the clothes of the TV queen who'd been a model in her day, so my girlfriend adorned herself in tight-fitting but authentic Versace, all ruffles and animal prints. 'Just because it's short on me that doesn't mean it's any less elegant,' she assured me from under the straight blonde wig that drove me crazy because it made her look like a cross between Doris Day and a builder. That lunch was a feast. We had spaghetti bolognese under the gaze of the immigrant great-grandfather with a gelled moustache who'd opened the restaurant at the beginning of the last century. We were about to become immigrants ourselves. The yacht arrived that day. Daniel had sent it, along with visas and passports for both of us. It took us to Montevideo. From there we went to Miami by plane, as one should. He'd changed our identities a bit: I ended up being Catalina Sánchez Quit and Cleo achieved one of her most impossible dreams: getting her name on her documents. Since then, finally and forever, her name has been Cleopatra Lobos. *Lobos*, meaning wolves. Sometimes when we argue, I tell her she's a whore right down to her last name: in Ancient Rome, a wolves' den was another way of saying a brothel. But she says it's impossible to offend her these days. 'Quity, my love, I've been through it all, nothing can humiliate me now. Especially not this moralistic fever that's come over you since we got to Miami. You wanted me even after you saw first-hand the whore I was, so don't come to me with this crap now, dear.' We left with a little bit of cash, some ten thousand dollars I'd saved and another five thousand that Daniel gave us. As Cleo likes to say, 'Money attracts money,' and here we are with a lot of money, two rich ladies in the developed world.

3. CLEO: 'IT WAS ALL THANKS TO THE VIRGIN MARY'

It was all thanks to the Virgin Mary
who changed my entire life:
the miracles started happening
and even the slum seemed alright.

Oh, Quity, if you'd only started the story at the beginning you'd understand things so much better. What's the beginning? There are loads of beginnings, my sweetness, because there are loads of stories, but I want to tell the story of this love of ours, which you don't remember too well, Quity. You tell some things like they happened and some of the other things, well, I don't know what you do, my love, you say all kinds of stupid stuff. So I'm going to tell our story myself. I'm going to record it for you, my darling, and you're going to add it to your story. Wait, wait, little Cleopatra just came in. What are you doing in here, my little dove? Didn't Mummy tell you to stay downstairs? Yes, go downstairs, sweetheart, let Mummy finish her work and then she'll come and play with you. Yes, okay, I'll come down and we'll play Barbies. Sorry, anyway, now I'm back, I'm going to turn off the phones and close the door so I can tell the story in peace.

I'm not going to be able to tell the whole of it: there are things I still don't know. I don't know if I even want to know them. It's not going to change my life, but I'm curious, and it eats away at me a bit, like being hungry or horny. It's just curiosity. I don't get what you don't understand about it. What drew Eve to the apple? You have no trouble pretending to be curious when you want to annoy me! How do I know what drew Eve to the apple, my love? They're red, they smell nice, she must have felt like biting into it. I don't think it's something I should really have to explain. Anyone ought to be able to understand curiosity – except you, Quity, since you're practically an extra-terrestrial. And don't play stupid, don't send me to ask the Virgin because I've already told you hundreds of times that the Virgin doesn't like it when I ask her about every little thing. She makes a face like she's annoyed, clams up and not even God could make her talk. Well, maybe God could make her talk. But the fact is, she gets her knickers in a twist if I ask her too many questions. I don't know why, maybe she gets sick of all us mediums, we're all chicks, we're probably too gossipy. Yeah, I know, guys can be gossipy too, maybe I *am* a male chauvinist, Quity, even though I refuse to accept my masculinity, according to you, who's not curious about anything because you don't give a shit about anything and also because you just go and make up whatever story suits you. The truth is I was never male, my dearest.

But I don't want to talk about that today. I want to talk about the beginning, and the question of whether or not I was ever male isn't the beginning of anything, I don't think. It started that day I saw you guys there in the slum. It was really early and you arrived all fresh and happy like you were ready for a picnic, you even had hiking boots and hiking trousers on, the kind of clothes you'd use to go on holiday to the jungle. You thought going into the slum was like going on safari. Well, how do I know what you thought, but you seemed not to realise we dressed like normal people, like everyone else, in work clothes, or clubbing clothes, or around-the-house clothes, not like you who showed up ready to hunt a bear or walk on some shifting sand dunes. Daniel was looking sophisticated. Such a handsome man. I liked Daniel when I saw him that day, those blue eyes and that silver hair of his just killed me. Well, Quity, you were no virgin yourself, and you know that before you I didn't want anything to do with chicks, I'd never gone beyond sucking some pussy when one of my more depraved clients wanted to pay extra for the show. But I'm not talking about that, I'm talking about Dani. I thought he was a cop because he was taking pictures and pretending not to the whole time we were eating breakfast, but he also looked too posh to be a cop. Also he was with you and I thought you were on the production crew of some TV show. You looked like one of those slutty chicks who come to the slum to film some documentary or buy some coke, a bit of a hot mess. I had you pegged from the start. And look at us now, my queen! Whoever would have imagined it? Two happy mums with a terrace overlooking the Caribbean and international fame! Ever since the Virgin's first miracle in the police station I knew my life was going to be charmed, but I never in a million years imagined I'd be here today, the mother of your daughter, in a mansion and on TV all day long. Well, I did imagine that when I was little: I wanted to be a showgirl and be on TV, I wanted to be on TV more than I wanted to be a showgirl actually. And did it work out? Yes and no. I'm on TV but I'm not a showgirl, I'm more like a sort of nun even though you say I still look a bit like a whore. Still, I know I'm famous because I can talk to the Virgin and not because of my tits, even though they're pretty big. For someone who claims to be straight, I have to say you went pretty crazy for them, and when I got these huge nipples that you love so much and that cost us a fortune to redo in Miami you made me feel like the wolf that nursed both Remus and Romulus.

Yes, Quity, my love, I realise I'm only on TV because of the Virgin and because of everyone that died, and because you wrote almost all the lyrics of the cumbia opera that shot me into the stratosphere of worldwide Latin stardom. And now you're writing this book and I imagine you selling it to Hollywood and some little Salvadoran boy playing me. No, the Virgin hasn't had a single complaint about it. She's been a star for two thousand years, you think she doesn't love fame? I don't know how, I guess it was etched on her eternal mind and her mortal heart and so she still loves it. It may seem impossible, she still enjoys fame even though she's been dead for like two thousand years! Oh, not dead, I meant she's been immortal for two thousand years. Your Greek gods loved fame too. And no, Quity, it's not that hard to believe they loved it if they made us, or if the ones who made them are the same as the ones who made us. Oh, you're so difficult. I don't even know why I love you; you never give me a break even for a second, as if I didn't have enough with little María Cleopatra, who you don't pay any attention to, my love, even though you had the privilege of carrying her in your womb. I know God made lizards too and you can't understand lizards even though we have the same father. I think I understand Juancho pretty well: ever since I changed his pool and started giving him organic frogs and Patagonian salmon he looks at me lovingly. He wants to be comfortable and eat well and be loved, does that sound so strange to you, silly billy? Everyone wants to be loved, even rocks want to be loved. And I'm not just spouting bullshit here. It's my turn and I'm going to keep recording my comments, Quity. You can write whatever you want but I want to tell my truth too. I know you never said I was stupid but in your book I come off like an idiot, so you're going to put all this that I'm saying in there too, my sweetness, and if you don't, you can take me out of your book completely. Or I'll add it in myself. I have the right to make myself heard.

So, that morning, I thought Dani looked like some posh police officer but since you were there too I thought you guys were from the TV or something and that you must be making a secret documentary. I don't know why you needed to be filming in secret, but then again, I didn't think it through. Anyway, I didn't really care because I knew I was going to end up on TV eventually. The Virgin told me that much, and then I was sure of it on the morning when the Virgin Mother disappeared because of Susana's howling and carrying on, do you remember? Yeah, I know you wrote about it, but I'm just remembering it now and I guess I'm asking more out of nostalgia. Because we've shared so many memories, because I don't even know how to think about myself without talking to you. Susana threw her wheelchair aside and jumped up howling, splashing through the mud like a little girl with her legs all cured, praising the miracle and swearing she'd give me a spot in the next season of her show. I got kind of pissed off about the shouting: 'Do you have to be so loud about it? The Virgin doesn't like it,' and sure enough, the Holy Mother disappeared without even giving me a kiss goodbye like she normally does. She just said, 'Pray, my daughter, and God will help thee and care for thee,' or something like that. In Spanish, too. The Virgin hardly speaks Spanish at all now we've moved her to Florida, have you noticed?

17

4. QUITY: 'THE VIRGIN SPOKE LIKE SOME MEDIEVAL SPANISH GIRL'

The Virgin spoke like some medieval Spanish girl and the days would always start with the first cumbia. Everyone said whatever they felt like saying using their own choice of syntax and together the songs created a cumbia language to tell all the different stories. I heard about love and gunshots, backstabbings and sex, happy cumbia, sad cumbia, angry cumbia all day long. Now I don't want to hear cumbia ever again. That's why we have the white living room, the bulletproof glass, the air conditioning. I write about what happened and nothing, or almost nothing, changes around me: my daughter grows noisily in another part of the house and Cleo gets older and confuses herself with one of the rich, bleached, useless ladies of Miami. Even though she's the religious one, I'm the monk in this family. Cleo lives surrounded by change, with the windows thrown open and constant shouting, the way we used to live back in the slum. We'd set up a communication system that used stolen mobile phones, but it was useless: the habit of spreading the word by shouting across the slum won out. 'Ginger's got new teeth', 'The cops are coming down the motorway', 'Jessica's got a new boyfriend', or whatever the news was, from shack to shack. The constant stream of information never let up, or if it did it was because someone had turned up at someone else's shack in person. Never mind what time – all it took was a package of sweets or crisps, salami and beer, and the party would start or continue. That's how it was: happiness radiated from the very heart of the slum. It might have looked like it was because of the Virgin and Cleo, but it was us, it was the power of us all coming together.

I know that now, but I can't take any noise at all these days. I think if someone played a cumbia at full volume right this second, I'd gun them down. I can't be around people, I almost never go out, I'm like the modern version of the madwoman in the attic: the lunatic in the bunker. Curiously enough, this isolation is the best indicator of adaptation to American society. I'm part of the Bunker Club, a group of sick nutjobs locked in incubators as hermetically sealed and impenetrable as they are self-sustainable. I could go two years without leaving and there are others who are equipped to be locked away for ten or twenty, but I always thought that once you lock yourself in, you never come back out. Like that monk from Cuzco who spent twenty years stuck in a cave painting pictures from hell, and you think, of course, what else would you paint if you were trapped in a cave for twenty years, and when he came out, he came out dead. I go outside sometimes, to feel the sun. I take little María Cleopatra to the beach and we make sandcastles and sand angels and she laughs, happy to have one of her mothers all to herself. I distance myself from her too: I think about our time on the island in the Paraná Delta where I slept away the better part of my pregnancy surrounded by mosquitoes and suffocating humidity. I can think about before, the slum, and after, our escape, but I can't remember the details, dates, names. I know I've forgotten a lot, my memory collapses under the weight of what I can't recall, but I remember Kevin with his feet in the water and his head in the mud and the mud full of blood and the colourless carp floating on the surface of the pond.

Our escape was supposed to be pretty much immediate. We thought we'd row to Uruguay, but in the end we stayed on the island for three months. I was always with Cleo and Cleo was always with the Virgin, that chunk of cement that occupies the centre of the living room still today, even if we are able to buy art after the success of our cumbia opera. The centre of our living room is an altar. I don't believe in the Holy Trinity or in the virgin wife, mother, sister and daughter, but I live with Cleopatra, my wife, the mother of my daughter. I love her and so I've come to terms with this trinity. We started out in March and we didn't end up leaving until the end of June. All this was almost two years after that first day Daniel and I had happily set off down the road to the slum.

We had no idea that that road was like the passageway to another dimension, the most important channel-change of our lives. Or at least of mine; I don't know if Daniel was able to change his. I don't think so. We'd stopped for coffee on the road... it must have been early November. I clearly remember the crowd of little slum children with white flowers spilling from their hands. They would throw themselves against the windshields shouting 'Jasmines! Jasmines! Don't you want some flowers, doll? Buy your girl a bouquet, boss, it's just some spare change.' I wanted some and Daniel liked the smell so the kid left with the change and his body in one piece. He was lucky, it's easy to get hit in these zealous sales attempts. Every once in a while the tarmac gets splattered with their guts and the cars don't stop and the kids end up flattened, like the dogs on the same roads.

It was early November when we first visited the slum, Daniel and I, together but united by what? What were the bonds that held us together? They were strong bonds and they endured, from the moment we met until his death. Was it something to do with that infantile faith he had in his

Kirlian photos? For the record, my aura is blue and 'blue is the colour of noble souls', as Daniel affirmed with unshakeable certainty. It was the kind of faith an engineer has in his equipment. Daniel needed the electronic sophistication of his Kirlian camera's lens in order to believe something else existed, to believe in goodness, and in a limitless colour, the colour blue. There was good in me, according to Daniel. And isn't that kind of certainty enough of a bond?

But it wasn't all aura with me and him. Our relationship had begun as a professional one: I was a crime reporter for a large newspaper and he worked for the Secretariat of Intelligence. We'd met when they'd sent me to cover a horrible case, the murder of a teenage girl from a poor family by a group of rich teenage boys. 'Homicide,' said Daniel, who didn't like small talk, 'is sometimes a necessary evil.' But to fill a girl up with coke only to then fill her up with come and empty her of blood, ripping her to shreds 'as if a pack of tigers had fucked a deer as they were eating it for breakfast', until she was almost dead, and then burying her when she was still almost alive, seemed to go beyond the realm of necessity to him. Also, I thought to myself, the boys' families were rich but not so rich as to be above the law – 'and besides, this isn't Ciudad Juárez,' Daniel added. He seemed genuinely offended. 'They had no reason to do something like this. There was no need: these little sons of bitches just gave in to gluttony, or worse, to lust, or worse still to the sin of killing for pleasure,' declared the stoical Daniel, who did however believe in killing when it wasn't for pleasure. This was over the first coffee of the hundreds we'd have together. We weren't linked only by his Kirlian photos: like me, he'd studied literature at university, and like me, he'd dropped out. To take up a job with the Secretariat, in his case. 'I picked the wrong path: I turned my life into a sad, boring spy novel when I really just wanted to write a thriller, not live one,' he told me that night in the bar, two or three years before the November morning that turned out to be the first day of what I now consider the rest of my life. At the time, I thought it might somehow lead to my return to literature as well. I too had wanted to be a writer and had studied classical literature, but I abandoned my artistic ambitions and the Greek language for the newspaper and the good coke I was guaranteed through close contact with the police. I lived to work and to snort blow and so my sources, my cops, my dealers, thieves, judges, lawyers and prosecutors became my friends, my lovers, my family. That was my life.

When Daniel told me the story of Cleopatra, I thought I'd found the perfect subject for the book that would allow me to apply for the hundred thousand dollars the Iberian New Journalism Foundation gave as an advance to fund the stories that interested them. And a transvestite who'd managed to organise the slum thanks to her communication with the Heavenly Mother, a dick-sucking daughter of Lourdes, a saintly whore with a cock to boot, would surely be of interest. And then I could quit the newspaper and go back to the beginning, to literature, the Greeks, the motionless maelstrom of translations and the dry violence of academic debate.

And in a way, that's what happened on that November morning when Daniel, who believed there was good in me, and I, who wanted to believe the same, went into the slum. November, the white flowers, the coke, the sunrise on the motorway, the writing, Daniel and his Kirlian camera, me and my Smith & Wesson, the bridges, the asphalt, the guts, the golf course adjacent to the slum; everything and everyone rolled down the green slope outside the shantytown and smashed into the grimy containment wall of El Poso, that dark, jumbled, shrill and oozing cluster of life and death.

5. QUITY: 'IT ALL STARTED
WITH THE COPS'

It all started with the cops
busting open my face
but the Holy Mother appeared
and healed me through her grace
and she told me I had to stop
spending my life sucking cock
so I quit my job as a trannie whore
and told the world it was She they should adore.

But even before sliding down into the slum from the
higher ground around the motorway like the rainwater that
left it constantly flooded, I'd seen Cleo looking so very pretty
and sounding so very eloquent on screen. Dani had copied
the surveillance videos from the El Poso slum along with
the criminal record of Sister Cleopatra, as they called her
back then. It was pretty illegal, supposedly only Intelligence
employees were allowed to see the surveillance and the tapes
were meant to be destroyed if there was no crime. Ever since
the walls of the shantytown had been studded with cameras,
the devotional routine of the 'Sister' had become more like
a talk show hosted by some daytime diva. Cleopatra – or
'Kleo', as she called herself when she used to advertise her
services, before God started talking to her – adopted, after

God started talking to her, the look of Eva Perón and a stage presence that rivalled that of Susana Giménez, all-time TV diva and Cleo's childhood obsession. The first records they had of her came from a hospital, a jail and a newspaper clipping. She was twelve years old, she was still called Carlos Guillermo and her father had almost beaten her to death 'for being a fucking faggot', as was explained in an article for the obscenely sensationalist newspaper *Crónica* published under the headline: *Homophobic Brutality: Father Nearly Kills Oldest Son for Wanting to Be Like Susana*. The press went to interview the boy at the hospital, and the TV diva was so touched when she found out how much the boy loved her that she invited him onto her show. That's when Carlos Guillermo was definitively transformed into Kleo, still on crutches but dancing delightedly with the feather boas the diva placed around his neck. A few years later Kleo re-entered the limelight, as a result of some changes made to the slum that meant the poorest of the poor were finally able to enjoy the latest technology as well as everyone else. If the rich had security cameras and walls, why couldn't they put up a wall and cameras around the shantytown? They deserved safety as much as anyone and desperately needed protection from the gang members who robbed even their own neighbours. This was the argument laid out by the middle and upper classes, politicians and the media. The gangs of teenage thieves didn't like it one bit. At first they splattered the cameras with paint, but the next day the cops would come in and take away the person they'd filmed vandalising. Wearing balaclavas like the good old Zapatistas didn't work either because the cops would just smash up someone's house until they gave names. In the end, they resigned themselves to sharing the spoils of their robberies with the police. The cameras continued filming, the videos began to circulate and Cleopatra enjoyed the attention. With her hair swept back like Evita, champion of the downtrodden, and a bounce in her step like Susana, the queen of TV, and as blonde as both of them, the 'transvestite saint', surrounded by a court of pimps, prostitutes, thieves in training and other transvestites, preached with one arm around the statue of the Virgin a grateful workman had erected for her on the field inside the shantytown. The Virgin's head was rather too large, and so was her nose. She was a bit rickety, with a cross in her right hand and a heart in her left. But Mary presided over the gatherings with her eyes turned skyward and a look of ecstasy on her face. 'Like she's being done from behind,' in the words of Jessica, Cleo's niece, who evidently thanked the heavens every time she had that experience. 'One night,' Cleopatra said, recounting the story of the Virgin's first miracle for her followers, 'the pigs raided the flat I was working in.' She'd done karate when she was a boy so she was able to knock down a couple of the cops in self-defence. Then she was taken to the police station. They cut the cables on the cameras and, with shouts of 'You goddam faggot, now you're going to see what it means to be a man', they beat her and gang raped her. The other prisoners joined in as well, clear evidence of the democratisation of the police force ever since they started making them go through police academy. Choking on her own blood and the semen of the entire police station, Cleo had a vision: the Virgin. 'She was divine, blonder than Susana, and dressed all in white. She looked like she was wearing a silk tunic. She wiped my face with a tissue she got from I don't know where, I think she had it up her sleeve, well, how should I know where she had it, enough with the stupid questions. So anyway, she sat me on her knee and told me not to worry, she was going to take care of me now and they weren't going to kill any more of her children, and who did they think they were. I had to change my life, she told me. It wasn't good for me to go around "copulating",

27

which means screwing, all day long, and I had to take care of myself. Since she was speaking so properly she sounded like Queen Sofía of Spain, and I thought it was funny. She asked me what I was laughing at and I told her and she's so good that she didn't get mad, she just laughed too and gave me a kiss on the forehead. She told me I was very sweet and she wanted me to marry her son, who'd take care of me like she would. And she started to tell me things that were going to happen and things that had already happened to me. It felt like she'd known me my whole life, as if we'd gone back in time and she'd been with me from when I was little, from when my dad almost killed me, and she cured me of everything, I didn't even have the limp any more when I woke up. The cops almost fainted: they'd left me for dead and I'd just got up like nothing had happened and told them to repent, that Jesus and the Virgin were going to forgive them if they repented. And so they came into the cell where they'd thrown me and saw everything all clean and perfect and me looking dazzling, like I'd spent the night on a feather bed with satin sheets. There I was eating the breakfast the Virgin had left me, tea with milk and sugar and pastries. They were shocked when they opened the door and saw me stand tall and waltz out like a queen, not a mark on me, like I was ready to step in front of the camera and appear on TV that very morning.'

6. QUITY: 'THE MORNING AFTER'

The morning after we watched the video, Dani and I rushed to the slum. He wanted to take a Kirlian photo of Cleo and I wanted to write the story of the year. I liked to drive north of the city, to see the river even if only in glimpses, to smell the water, to slow to the rhythm of the landscape as we got close to the Delta. But that day we didn't make it all the way to the river. We exited the motorway as soon as we saw the shantytown. It was built on the lowest ground: everything sloped gently downwards the closer you got to it, except the quality of life, which didn't slope but rather dropped off sharply in the last few inches before the wall – a wall whose advertising potential the municipality hadn't overlooked. The wall served as a mirror for the wealthy neighbours, their last line of protection: instead of seeing the slum, they saw only themselves in the ads plastered to the wall, people on top of the world with their expensive mobile phones, cars, perfumes and holidays.

Shame all those images of prosperity had to be inter-rupted by the grimy gates of poverty. The archway over the entrance was charming, with colourful letters that read 'Welcome to El Poso' and some painted cement doves, intended, I suppose, to be holding the sign up with their beaks, but looking more like they'd flown into a window. Little balls with wings plastered to the corners of the sign.

On each side of the entryway was a security booth that bore various layers of decoration. The first layer was the requisite dark blue of all the booths; the second included the rooster of the Buenos Aires Police Department's shield; the third, redheaded mermaids, a yellow submarine, the baby Jesus walking on a blue puddle, green fish and water lilies, all with eyes and smiling out from the dark blue background. The other layers of decoration consisted of graffiti, little cocks for everyone, including the baby Jesus. If it hadn't been for the cocks and the smell of shit, you'd have had the impression you were entering a Catholic preschool in a poor neighbourhood. The security guard looked like just another decoration, a surprised octopus poking his head out of the booth's window. Intelligence and press, the badges Daniel and I carried, gave us right of passage.

'Go ahead, sir. Have a nice day, sir.' The octopus respected hierarchy even though he was dying of curiosity.

'Are you coming to see the Sister, sir?'

'What's your name, Officer?'

'John-John Galíndez, Inspector.'

'Are you the artist, Galíndez?' Dani asked, mischievously nodding toward the elaborately painted booth.

'Negative, sir. That would be Jessica, the Sister's niece. Would you care for a drink of *mate*, young lady?'

'Yes, thanks, John-John. Busy day?'

'No, not really… Ever since the Virgin's been around, the slum's been pretty quiet. Very quiet. The only problems we have now are with the Condors, the private security paid for by the rich neighbours. Even the cokeheads get up early to listen to the Sister, she's a comfort to us all. It's pretty incredible. You'd never know it, Inspector, but, and my apologies to the young lady here, the Sister used to be a bit of a bitch. She worked in a whorehouse here in San Isidro, near the cathedral. She was expensive. For the posh set, you know.' Galíndez lowered his voice and looked from side to side before continuing, 'They say she was the bishop's lover.'

'Isn't she a bit old for the bishop's tastes, Officer?'

'Well… I don't know, I'm not a reporter, you'd know better than me. But that's what they say around here, and you never know, there's an exception to every rule, isn't there?' the officer answered. 'Besides, Cleopatra was young before she was old.'

'And before she was Cleopatra…', Daniel ventured and the cop chuckled, warming up and almost certainly thinking: 'This is my kind of guy.' Then he started talking nonstop. He'd worked this precinct for eight years, and although he hadn't been at the station on the day of the miracle, he'd witnessed other ones. 'The Sister forgave us all,' he repeated over and over, shocked that a victim could forgive such terrible things as the ones he'd done. He was right that any self-respecting person would consider these violations unforgivable, but Cleopatra says I'm bitter and that if everyone thought like me we'd all end up killing each other. The officer continued with his story: 'It's unbelievable, but I saw the miracle too. Cleopatra used to have one leg shorter than the other from when her father had beaten her to a pulp. Just imagine, he was a police officer, Sergeant Ramón Lobos, though later he was sacked for keeping more than his share of a payoff. When his son turned out like that – different, let's say – he wanted to kill him. There's still a lot of prejudice in the force.'

I think it was a November morning, like I said, but I remember it being cold. We stepped inside John-John's booth and he carried on serving *mate* and explaining the prejudices of the force: 'In the academy they give us classes on human rights. In the test everyone writes that it's bad to discriminate against the poor, the fags, the Jews, the Bolivians, and then, as soon as they can stick it to them, they stick it to them. But not here, not any more: we don't even beat the poor anymore, we have to defend them from the Condors.' And he wasn't lying: it was common knowledge that the Condor Private Security Agency had taken all the illicit side businesses away from the cops, who then ended up defending the people in the slum because they needed them as human resources to go out and make the dirty money for them. The cops were desperate; they needed someone to go out and make the cash that was scarcer than it had ever been before, and someone had to stand up to their colleagues in private security, the Condors. 'Led by that crazy arsehole the Beast,' John-John declared. 'He says God speaks to him too but no one's ever seen him perform a single miracle, unless you count burning a hooker who doesn't pay up and then keeping the money that's supposed to go to everyone. That can't be something our Lord Jesus Christ would tell him to do.'

The last thing he told us was that after Cleopatra's first miracle even the police captain repented: he ended up sobbing, 'like a baby, at the Sister's feet'. Pretty much everyone does. Even I still do every once in a while, in my bunker in Miami. But way before all that ever happened and I ended up here, we left the security booth and went into the shantytown. And well before the shantytown meant anything more to me than a sad detail of the landscape alongside the motorway that took me to the Delta, I'd heard of the Beast, former cop, head of the Condors, the most ruthless private security agency in greater Buenos Aires. The Beast, lord of prostitution in the outskirts of the capital and right-hand man of El Jefe Juárez, the country's most powerful businessman. I'd never spoken to the Beast. I'd just caught a glimpse of him now and then. But I'd had to finish one of his jobs once and that moment changed me. It pushed me onto the other side, the side of my sources, the people I used to interview. It also brought me closer to Daniel.

7. QUITY: 'I'D BEEN WORKING FOR HOURS AND HOURS'

I'd been working for hours and hours that day, covering the kidnapping of a businessman in the town of Quilmes, south of Buenos Aires. I ended up having dinner with his future widow and his soon-to-be-fatherless children as they waited for the captors to call. They didn't call and it got late, and it was around three in the morning when I set off home.

I drove slowly through the town centre because I'd had a bit to drink. I passed the first part of the slum that surrounded the motorway, going even slower then because there's always the odd horse or drunk around there, and when I got to the last five hundred yards before the entrance ramp and was about to speed up again, everything went black. All the lights in the area went out, yellowish lights that blinked from the windows and holes in the shacks, hung from extension cords strung from ceiling to ceiling like pumpkins from a miserable Halloween or Christmas decorations from the holiday from hell. Everything went silent, too. The only sounds were the deep, muted roars of the cars on the motorway above, brightly lit and as tauntingly distant as the shore to a drowning man.

I turned off my headlights. They weren't doing much anyway, and besides, as everyone knows, being the only visible thing is very similar to being the only target. I took my .38 Smith & Wesson from the glove compartment and put it on the passenger seat, not thinking it would really do any good. Although the motorway punctuated the blackness and added a touch of normality to the scene, there was a stillness and silence that seemed almost tangible, and more than a band of teenage thieves, I feared I'd be attacked by an army of zombies. My lungs and my brain felt squeezed and I was left with only one idea: to get the hell out of there. There wasn't a soul on the street, you couldn't even hear the cry of a baby or a cumbia beat or the rattle of a cart or the bark of a dog and the only thing that moved, dark and slow, was my car, as if I were the only thing that existed. But everyone was still there. Turning off the lights and holding your breath is the shantytown's way of saying there are no witnesses, that no one wants to have anything to do with what's happening or even see or hear it take place.

What was happening occurred a few seconds after the blackout, like thunder and lightning in reverse order: first the sound, a terrifying howl that sent me into the kind of animal alert mode that made my hair stand on end. All I managed to do was press the accelerator and grab the revolver, but that meant letting go of the wheel and I ended up on the curb, making a thunderous, metallic racket, the only noise besides the howling, as a lamppost crunched against the car's back door. Everything else was black and still like an empty stage. Then came the light: a human flame running a kind of epileptic race, with movements that seemed impossible for a human body and a heart-rending shriek, running like someone falling, the torso plunging over the feet, contorting with the heat of the undulating flames that were burning the body alive.

I saw her fall. Because she was wearing high heels I guessed she was a woman. I saw her fall thinking that you couldn't witness a fall like that without doing something and I considered my options, for maybe two, five, ten seconds.

Until the urge became desperate, to move, to grab my coat and jump out of the car. I was so coked-up I thought the cold of the night would shatter me to pieces like I was made of glass, but I wasn't shattered by the cold and I wasn't shattered by the smell of burnt flesh. I wasn't shattered when I hugged my red coat around the woman who moaned and howled and wheezed like a dying whale and ground her teeth like in Dante's *Inferno*. I wasn't shattered when I sat on the ground and curled her onto my lap like she was a baby so I could put out the flames, and I wasn't shattered when I looked into her eyes, which were still alive in her carbonised face, telling her not to worry, that it was all over, lying that everything was going to be alright. I wasn't shattered when I put the barrel of the .38 against her temple as I rocked her to and fro. Smearing myself with the slimy flesh and the fluids of her barbecued body didn't shatter me and shooting her, bathing in the spray of blood and brains that came out of her head, didn't shatter me either.

In the soundless slum, my bullet was like a firecracker in a metal barrel, like my heart pounding in my empty body. The sound broke something, like the earthquake that ripped the curtains of the temple when Christ was killed. After firing the shot, my arm flew into the air like a railway crossing barrier and I left my life behind me forever.

The noise of the bullet reminded me of the danger. No one else had appeared yet, and I adopted the first of many shantytown survival strategies that would mark my behaviour from that night on. I walked to my car without making a sound, as if my silence could somehow erase the boom as I put her out of her misery. Once I got into the car and the door was firmly closed I hit the accelerator, pulling the lamppost down behind me as I ploughed up the ramp to the motorway. In the rearview mirror I could see first the spotlights of the van from *Crónica TV* focusing on the girl and then the blue lights of the police cars, which got there second. But I didn't stop. I didn't stop until I got to my flat, until I was looking at myself in the bathroom mirror whilst shitting for hours like I'd eaten the entire body of the woman I'd just killed.

I was black all over with a crust on my face and hands like I'd hugged an overcooked rack of ribs, and on my right arm was the spray you get after suicides or killings at point-blank range. I'd seen it before on plenty of dead bodies, and had it pointed out to me by plenty of forensic investigators wanting to prove their hypotheses, that trail of spots with irregular quantities of blood and brain and powder. Every part of me was shaking with fear, even my blood. I showered, cleaning myself with a kitchen sponge and washing-up liquid, with clothes detergent, with shower gel and bath foam. I thought about burning my clothes but I didn't want to see fire even on the stove so I shoved everything, down to the underwear I'd had on, into some bleach, and since my heart was still booming like firecrackers in a safe, I took half a box of Xanax and got into bed and sat there with the revolver, which I also wiped with bleach. I was feeling as crazy as Macbeth with my bloody scabs, but being from the twenty-first century has its advantages: modern pharmacology can anesthetise even the most anxious of killers. I slept the entire day and had nightmares and when I woke up I saw the messages from Daniel telling me what he knew. Next to the girl they'd found a piece of paper with cut-out letters from the newspaper glued to it, words made with different sizes, typefaces and colours. A new genre, said Dani; a kind of evil, biblical pop art. It read: 'It is a burnt offering by fire as an appeasing fragrance for Yahweh.' The theory that had caught on was that it was a mafia-related killing but they didn't know who to attribute it to, according to the media. But everyone knew. Daniel knew and I knew as soon as I heard the verse from Leviticus. It couldn't be anyone but the Beast.

Daniel came to my house and gave me a summary of all the information he had. The girl was Paraguayan, her name was Evelyn, she was sixteen years old and Interpol had been looking for her for three years, ever since she disappeared from her home in Ypacaraí. According to the newspapers, it was suspected she'd been kidnapped by a network of human traffickers. Daniel was sure of it. I was too.

'Someone put her out of her misery,' he said. I could hardly breathe as I drank my whisky and looked at the photos of Evelyn that Dani had taken from the Interpol files. I'd sworn myself to silence: killing someone, however merciful the intention, is still homicide and homicides get long jail sentences in any justice system. To tell anyone was to turn yourself in. But it could also serve as some form of absolution, gaining an accomplice to share the weight of the death, to receive support, the freedom of falling voluptuously into another person's hands. I don't know, maybe it was just verbal diarrhoea brought on by my drunkenness. I never have been able to drink without talking too much and I've never managed to get through a difficult situation without a bottle of J&B on hand. I'd chosen my confidant well: Dani hugged me, took Kirlian photos to show me my soul was as blue as ever, poured me some more whisky and some for himself too, skipped the rest of the workday and had his own bout of verbal diarrhoea, giving free rein to his mystic-electronic deliriums, telling me that there were four different states matter could exist as, solid, liquid, gas and bioplasma. It didn't bother him when I said that in that case water wouldn't be matter because in school they taught us it had only three states. He told me how in 1939 the Russian engineer Semyon Davidovich Kirlian was carrying out an electrotherapy experiment. You mean electroshock, I said, but he carried on without answering. The important thing, he said, is that the Russian received a shock when he accidentally touched an electrode. He happened to have a piece of photosensitive paper nearby and rested his hand on it and took a picture, and when he developed it he saw haloes of light around his fingers. Apparently this light comes from the atoms that make up the human body, which possess a nucleus of protons, neutrons and many other subatomic particles, and electrons spin around this nucleus in an elliptical orbit at a speed of almost 200,000 miles a second. I don't remember how exactly, but Daniel said all this was related to the soul: the colours of the aura reveal the psyche, he told me, and it seemed he took as a given the relationship between psyche and soul. He began to stammer and chew his words as he made an effort to maintain his composure and showed me the photos he'd taken, bluer that day than before Evelyn even. 'Blue,' he stuttered, 'is the colour of good, Quity.' Then he showed me photos of his own aura, or maybe it was his psyche or his soul, I didn't quite understand if it was all the same to him or if they were three different things. There was nothing more than a bit of shy, greyish colour around Daniel's hand. This was because, as he began to tell me an inch from the end of the bottle, he had also killed. But in his case it had been revenge, not euthanasia. He repaid my confession with his own and we were each left in the other's hands. He cried as he spoke, blubbering, swigging whisky from the bottle and wetting his shirtfront with what spilled from his mouth. He'd had a daughter. She looked just like him only beautiful, he said. She was a good Catholic girl who cared about the earth, she was studying to become a vet and she did charity work in the slums, castrating and immunising pets for free. She wasn't proud of her father's job. 'I didn't mind,' he said. Daniel looked out for her: he'd bought her a flat, sent cops by the shantytowns the days she was working there and even drummed up a team of volunteers to help her.

He would have liked to have spent more time with her, to have lived with her, he deeply regretted having missed her childhood. He didn't tell me what had happened, but he wasn't there for her. She, Diana was her name, had been a bright light. Until one day some son of a bitch killed her. He kidnapped her, tortured her and raped her, and then he shot her when he got bored. The bottle was empty now and it was impossible to tell if what stained Daniel's clothes was whisky, tears or piss, because that night he also pissed himself. It was around the time of his daughter's death that he'd discovered Kirlian photography and been able to prove the existence of the spirit and with the existence of the spirit the existence of God and Justice, but despite this he'd been unable to resist getting revenge. Evidently, it wasn't the first time he'd killed someone. 'But before, I'd never had proof God existed, Quity.' Even with that proof and everything, when he found the motherfucker he took it upon himself, personally, and slowly, to dismember him. But he didn't feel any better afterwards, he explained. His daughter was dead and it was already too late for anything.

He didn't talk any more after that. He took a shower and put on the pyjamas the last guy who'd been more or less my boyfriend had left at my house. He put his clothes in the wash, cleaned the floor, came to my bedroom and hugged me like a father all night long. It was the start of a great friendship. For a long time I talked only to him and only when we saw each other in person.

I asked for psychiatric leave from work and easily met all the requirements, then isolated myself in my flat, looking in the mirror nonstop, searching my face for that look I used to search for in the murderers I interviewed. I spent months thinking about that girl, her shitty life and its even shittier ending. All stories end in death, but they'd fucked that girl every day, every day and inside out. They'd beaten her, they'd stripped her till she was left with nothing of her own, not time, not a single fold of her body. They'd taken away all her dignity, all of herself, until she was nothing but a thin shell they could rip open with their cocks. That they hadn't stripped her completely bare could be seen by the fact she'd tried to escape. That was the reason for the fire: the Beast had done it before to two or three girls who'd tried to run away.

The fact I hadn't put the gun in her mouth was a small consolation at least, as was the fact I'd rocked her, and put out the fire, and hugged her. She would have gone on suffering, she had no face, she had hardly any skin and the infections would have ended up killing her, but that's not why I killed her. I shot her simply because I couldn't stand to see so much suffering. I can still remember the fear in her eyes as she looked at me and the way she grabbed my hand with her grilled one when I pulled the trigger. I should've called an ambulance. But I was afraid the guys who'd set her on fire would show up before it arrived and I didn't want to waste a second. So I killed her and took off.

Afterwards I spoke to some of the forensic investigators I knew and saw Evelyn's body in the freezer, half-carbonised but clean. What wasn't burnt was beautiful, the body of a young woman, made to live, like everyone is. The doctors told me she would have died anyway, her left hand had been fused to her torso and she'd been so charred that her guts had started to come out. They couldn't figure out what the hell she'd been burnt with, the state of the body was similar to that of corpses pulled from fiery plane crashes. 'Someone put her out of her misery,' said Luis, the chief of forensics, and he made me feel a bit better even though I knew I could never go back to the other side, the other world, where people live life oblivious to the mini-Auschwitzes you get every five hundred feet in Buenos Aires. Evelyn was my one-way ticket, my entry into the slum. I killed her and she made me one of them.

8. QUITY: 'I WENT INTO THE SLUM'

I went into the slum a year and a half later, one day in November. It was very early, around eight in the morning – Daniel and I were assuming Sister Cleopatra would have rediscovered mornings after giving up her nocturnal lifestyle. It had rained a lot the day before and the slum was crawling back to life after the flood. We were sunk so deep in the mud that we seemed to be emerging from it, like the first creatures to be made by the god of the Virgin who talked, and still talks, to Cleopatra.

The centre of El Poso was flooded. When it rained there were no kids playing there, the Virgin didn't speak to anyone and the paths to the Lord could only be travelled by boat. The pampa grasslands may have natural highs and lows, but their geography is really determined by the social pyramid. Water always flows downwards to the lower ground, that much is obvious – and what's even more obvious is that down on the lower ground are the slums. Rains wash away the poorest shacks and even drown people from time to time. As far as I can recall, that morning the only victims of shipwreck were boxes of wine, syringes, plastic bottles and nappies. There were no dead bodies. We, the people who were alive, talked in groups, tapping along to the rhythm of the cumbia in the background while we waited for the Sister to emerge from the glare of the shantytown's proletariat;

those heads of spiky hair gleaming with gel, colourful belts, expensive sportswear and sparklingly clean trainers. The guys looked like ballerinas: they tiptoed across the mud, stepping only on rocks or sticks to preserve the immaculate shine of their shoes. The kids ran around and played tag despite their mothers howling at them to keep out of the shit on the ground. Some men laughed quietly with their mouths open, looking at the women, and the women laughed too, but they covered their open mouths with the automatic gesture of the flirtatious toothless. I was thinking about God, bread and toothlessness when Susana, the legendary TV diva herself, appeared, floating in mid-air. It was no miracle: her bodyguards were carrying her wheelchair so it wouldn't sink into the mud. I should be very clear at this point: El Poso was a swamp of shit. Susana, old as the hills and no longer surprised or frightened by anything, asked them to place her wheelchair between the wealthy ladies who'd come to hear the service and the cumbia star, a man from the slum who'd stayed in the slum, all of them flamboyantly dressed according to diverse models of extravagance originating in Miami.

The 'little sisters', Cleopatra's former co-workers, rushed back and forth, carrying away bags of rubbish and bringing improvised tables on their backs like the good, industrious and heavily made-up drag queens they were. There were bonfires and fat ladies beside the bonfires. That combination, bonfire and fat lady, released a charming scent of *mate* and toast; the air smelled like breakfast at home that morning when Cleopatra finally appeared carrying some jars. 'It's orange marmalade' were the first words I heard her say without the mediation of cameras and microphones. 'It's super-homemade, I made it with my own hands and the oranges are from the trees in the neighbourhood.' She leaned against the cement breasts of the large-headed Virgin and beamed as one by one people came up to present her with gifts or express their love for her. She giggled and bounced up and down like a little girl, like she still does today despite her crow's feet and despite all the deaths. Both of them, Cleo and our daughter, bounce up and down when they're happy, for example when I give the girl a new Barbie or Cleo a new bottle of perfume. That morning I could never have imagined that the smell of home and Cleopatra would stay in my life for ever.

So, Cleo was leaning on the Virgin and graciously accepting eggs, an iPhone, clothes, a red hen. The Virgin's medium let out a booming laugh: 'Oh, Gladys, come and see this chicken, she looks just like you, and she talks like you too!' We all laughed; they really did look alike. 'We'll call it Gladina,' Cleo decreed. 'Perfect, and I'll keep the eggs,' answered the red-haired Gladys. 'Yeah, let someone else do the laying for once, Ginger.' The gifts kept on coming: a silk blouse, ten baguettes, boxes of rice, a Louis Vuitton handbag. Cleo bounced up and down for practically five minutes straight when the elderly diva, her patroness, gave her a puppy. 'Oh, Sue, thank you, thank you, you shouldn't have, he's so adorable, what is it, it's a boy, right? Girls! What should we call him? Let's call him Gauchito. Oh, you're going to be swimming in ladies around here. And look, he's got a little collar. He's had all his shots. Great, because this one's classy and around here the classy ones catch the nastiest diseases.' The mad mystic paused, and then added: 'Well, we catch those nasty diseases too, but we're used to it.' Then, with a practicality that surprised me and continues to surprise me in a person who speaks with celestial beings, Cleo told us that God loved us, that through God we could love each other, and that we should have breakfast. It was time and it was freezing cold, and first things first. We could always pray later. Under the Sister's gaze, everyone was happy and friendly. People shouted out jokes and told stories. They felt like they were part of something. I didn't know what it was but they made me feel part of it too. A little boy, three years old, pointed to the bulge of my gun under my sweater and shouted 'Bam!' then threw himself on the ground and played dead, laughing and awaiting my approval. I was a little surprised by that level of understanding in such a little kid, but El Poso was the kingdom of eternal youth: no one dies of old age, they die of curable illnesses or unnecessary bullets. The boy jumped up, laughing, and I laughed with him, stroking his head as he hugged my legs. It was Kevin. He ate breakfast on my lap, happy as could be. I gave him a sweet I had in my purse and he gave me a kiss and I wanted to take him home and feed him sweets forever like the witch from Hansel and Gretel, not so I could eat him but so he'd give me kisses and be happy forever.

Dani was doing what he'd gone there to do: with his mouth full of toast, he was taking pictures. He had his Kirlian camera connected to his wrist PC so no one really noticed his incessant clicking. 'Quity, look at this,' he'd say about once a minute. 'It looks like the Strait of Messina: it's the biggest and bluest aura I've ever seen in my life,' he said, referring to the colour of Cleopatra's soul. 'Hallelujah, brother, she must really be a saint then.' He was overjoyed, he really believed that the lights he photographed were the soul, and that souls really existed. As further evidence, he insisted once again on showing me the photo of his soul, a dull grey thing with black spots. Daniel is a bastard, and he knows it. 'Blessed are those who understand their world,' I remember thinking as I watched a statue of the popular saint Deceased Correa pass by in the arms of a transvestite who looked like she'd been a bouncer in her previous life. Later on I found out that among transvestites there were the ones called to it innately and the ones forced into it out of necessity. The ones who'd known it forever began preparing early: they never did those 'macho jobs that would ruin the body of any lady', as Cleo explained to me later, still in the slum, when I was recording practically every word that came out of her mouth.

The transvestite carrying the statue of the Deceased was one of the ones who'd come to this lifestyle later and out of necessity. The Correa must have been the work of the same sculptor who'd made the Virgin, since she was equally scrawny and large-headed. In just a few minutes the field was flooded with a tide of saints: as in a kind of funeral procession, like colourful mummies, the saints rolled out, lying on the solid backs of the transvestites, nuns with exaggerated tits, themselves just as colourful, the whole scene seeming plucked from some ancient temple. Although they'd dressed with the discretion required for a sacred act, the shantytown trannies are like bats: they live life dressed for the night. Not even Cleo could do without her tight-fitting sparkle. She's better at it now, having learnt to wear mourning attire, dark knee-length dresses, veils, low heels, and even white trainers. But that morning, the morning of the scrawny, large-headed saints advancing like corpses toward a funeral pyre on the backs of girls as strong and exuberant as bulls, Cleo had yet to leave the world of necessity. She'd not yet enjoyed wealth and she hadn't learned discretion, that attribute which certain kinds of powerful people like to show off.

I'm not exaggerating: the Virgin and all her lesser saints looked like plaster sarcophagi modelled on malnourished teenage girls or extra-terrestrials of the kind NASA hides in some corner of this beautiful country. It was obvious that their deformed shapes were due to the sculptor's clumsiness. However, it was also obvious that he could have chosen many other varieties of deformity: feet as large as those of Patagonian tribes, fat bodies, super-long torsos or tiny heads, to list just a few, so it made one wonder: why such weak bodies and such disproportionately large heads? Was it some kind of slum realism? Maybe the sculptor was trying to say that the kingdom of heaven was all in the head, and it was there and nowhere else that the first would be last and the last would be first. Or maybe he was trying to imply that the disproportion was necessary to express the hopes of the poor, so mistreated, so downtrodden, so humiliated and yet still ready to believe in the possibility of salvation: the sculptor, the trannies, the girls, the toothless fat women, the teenage thieves and the builders gathered there in El Poso were all convinced the Virgin was going to protect them.

Dani and I watched it all ironically. It took me months to lose that idiotic perspective; the slum pantheon was like a party for two dickhead outsiders like Dani and me at that time. The popular saint Gauchito Gil, in his red horse-riding attire, elicited comments from us such as: 'Oh, has he been canonised?' 'I don't think so, Dani. When the Church is asked to canonise thieves, it prefers the kind that rob from the poor.' 'You're right: Jesus even said as much, render unto Caesar the things which are Caesar's.' 'Yes, but Caesar was alive and he must have had an idea of what should be done with the money. Now, Saint Martín, Roca, Mitre and Sarmiento, they might have founded this country but now they're long gone, so what the hell kind of good does the cash do them? It's definitely not going on the trains named after them, that's clear enough if you've been on one lately.' Catalina de Siena, patron saint of Rome, had been sculpted in great detail: she seemed to be kneeling down and eating what looked like a drumstick with five human toes tacked onto it like a bad punchline. 'Was she a cannibal, Dani?' 'No, don't you see there's a leaf of lettuce there too? She didn't eat anything else. The wedding ring she wore was made from Christ's foreskin, which, according to the saint, Jesus himself gave her when he took her as a wife. She said King David had played at the wedding and the Holy Mother performed the ceremony.' 'So, whose feet is she sucking on there?' 'Some sick person, she sucked the pus from their wounds to become comfortable with the wounds of Christ, her husband.' 'Oh, *l'amour...*'

Saint Pantaleon was a kind of monument to the tortured. Dani, who knew about him as well, told me the story: 'He was a charitable doctor who treated the poor. He converted to Christianity, then the Romans got onto him and gave him the routine punishment for members of annoying religious sects. But it didn't work: first they set him on fire but nothing happened, it was like the saint was made of asbestos. Then they tried molten iron and the good doctor shook it off like it was sand. They must've thought that if fire didn't work then maybe water would, so they held his head underwater for ten hours. The philanthropist emerged singing psalms. They threw him to the lions, the Romans' favourite spectacle at the time, but the beasts spat him out whole. They tortured him on the rack and he bent but didn't break, they stuck a sword in him and the quack took it as coolly as if they were serving him breakfast. The Romans persevered: they knew a state that doesn't finish its punishments is a dead state. When they tried to decapitate him, his head did separate from his body and Pantaleon finally died, but the miracles didn't end there: what spurted from his neck wasn't blood but milk. But you know how contradictory miracles can be – that doesn't stop the Royal Monastery of the Incarnation in Madrid displaying a relic of his blood, which is liquefied every year on the anniversary of the martyrdom of the blood's original owner.'

Saint Malverde was loaded down with packages of narcotics and carrying more weapons than Rambo. This story was one I knew: 'He's the patron saint of the Mexican narcos. He must've performed some miracle because all the drug mules pray to him for protection before they smuggle blow into the US. I don't think he's canonised but that doesn't take away from his powers: the last time I went to New York I almost turned into a statue myself; half the city was covered in snow and it was the middle of summer.'

As Daniel and I chatted, Kevin went on eating everything left on the table, which was a lot. He laughed and lifted up his shirt to show his belly every once in a while. The cumbia blared, the kids were dancing with Gladys, the redhead trannie who looked like the hen, and everyone else was shouting and laughing. That mystic breakfast seemed more like the wedding of two alcoholics. I don't know what I'd pictured or if I'd even pictured anything at all, but it certainly wasn't a country fair transposed to a slum. When even Daniel was moving his feet, they turned down the music and we all moved to the centre of the field, which was as clean as a middle-class living room now thanks to the sisters' work. Cleo sat down beside the statue once again. When I joined the circle of cement saints I was surprised to see a kind of large doll wearing armour. Daniel confirmed my suspicions: 'Yes, it's Joan of Arc.' Of course, because she was a bit of a cross-dresser too. The English burnt her for breaking her oath never to dress like a man again… The god they had back then was older, more like Zeus, and he was more sympathetic to France and wanted that idiot Charles VII to be king at all costs. That's why he sent some voices to that young woman who then transformed into an impressive general: so they could win a few battles. It didn't even enter God's head to bring the Hundred Years' War to an end. He was having too much fun watching, like his cousins on Olympus during the Trojan Wars.

9. QUITY: 'EVERYONE PRAYED'

Everyone prayed. They all knew the prayer and they said it aloud, eyes closed. I didn't join in. I knew the Hail Mary but I'd never been able to pray, and I couldn't then. I remember the impotence I felt as the chorus took a breath of filthy air and filled it with an 'Our Lord is with you' that filtered into the shacks through the holes in the sheet metal, a 'blessed art thou' that caressed the cans filled with geraniums and a 'pray for us sinners' that echoed against everything that had been born and was already decomposing with the brazenness of life in El Poso, 'now and at the hour of our death, amen'. Cleo still swears that the Virgin did her bit and prayed for us and continues to pray for those of us that died. I'm not fooled by Cleo or her Virgin: God is an ancient invention, made in the image of a tyrant, and like a tyrant he gives free rein to his fury when he feels like it. And there's no prayer that'll change that.

'Hi, Auntie' – despite the leopard-print lycra that must have been nearly suffocating her and the wine and pills that made it hard for her to articulate, Jessica hadn't lost her composure. 'Now we're all here we can begin,' said Cleopatra, and they began right then and there and I thought they'd never finish. Even Daniel prayed. Even Kevin. He blubbered fragments of the prayer from time to time and then looked up at me like he was expecting applause. That's all that was happening: they prayed and I listened. I was shocked that they thought anyone other than me was listening to their 'Our Lord is with you, Mary'. But later I understood: no god was listening to them but they were listening to themselves and they were listening together and it was that joining of forces that mattered. Even the illiterate in Argentina know the line from *Martín Fierro* that goes 'Brothers should stand by each other because this is the first law'.

After a while I stopped thinking and let myself be lulled by the Hail Marys, and I remembered myself in my God phase. A little girl in a white tunic with long hair that had been curled in front, at my communion party, on a hot day. I'd been hoping for something that didn't happen, I don't really know what, some kind of ecstasy I guess. My first communion wafer had been a disappointment just like a few years later my first drugs would be a disappointment, though I have to say I tried harder with coke than I'd ever tried with God. It was a question of literature: for a long time I found the beatniks much easier to get into than Saint Augustine. Yes, it was a very hot day, probably December 8th, the Feast of the Immaculate Conception. My mum threw a party for it, as is the custom. My aunt and my cousins and my neighbours came and I don't know who else. I could ask my mum if I cared but what I actually care about is that I never understood catechism at all. If he was actually God, how could he let those things happen to him? I'm a more basic creature than God, and I can't understand how someone who has the power to stop it would put themselves through torture.

'That's yucky,' I said to Kevin, who shook me from my musings as he made to bury himself in the mud. 'You can't put your hands in there, it's dirty.' I thought he was going to start crying so I balled up a piece of paper and he started kicking it around. It never fails. Sainthood was as much of a mystery to me as catechism. I briefly entertained the fantasy of going to work as a missionary in Africa, but more because of Tarzan than for the prestige of travelling the world to please some useless god. Death was far away for me and God just seemed like someone you could wish out loud to. I don't think I ever wished for so much that I needed to make up another person to wish to. I don't know why we remember some things and not others, or how associations are made, but I'm certain that I suddenly became aware, right as I was thinking about wishing and God, of a certain smell, the smell of Jonas, my dealer and my lover. And I remember being turned on. 'I have you in my sights,' he said. 'Then shoot,' I answered. Talking wasn't our strong suit. He hugged me from behind and I felt his body pulsing like mine. 'You can't let your guard down like that.' Sometimes I manage it, feeling happiness in my body. Sometimes. What was he doing there?

'What are you doing here?' he asked me first.

'I came to meet Cleopatra.'

I was happy to see him, and whenever I saw him I couldn't keep my hands off him. Kevin brought us back to the present before we could start making out right there in the shit-laden mud without any regard for the small crowd that was still reciting Hail Marys all around us. 'Water,' Kevin said. 'You want a sip of Coke, Kevin?' The boy smiled, 'Coke,' and Jonas handed him the bottle he had in his hand. 'Cleopatra is my aunt.'

'What a religious family. Your mum was some sort of mystic too, right?'

'Yeah, but Cleopatra is my dad's sister.'

'He must be proud.'

'He is now. Before, he'd always say crap like, "In this family we accept anyone, even cokeheads, but not fags." The night of the miracle a guy who works with him was in lockup at the police station. He told him what happened and it got him thinking. "That crazy bitch Cleopatra in El Poso," he said after a while, "must be my faggot brother Carlos Guillermo." He was very upset by her story. He came to tell her he was sorry and offered to get revenge on the guys who'd raped her. Cleopatra told him there was no need. She said she had to forgive them: they hadn't taken either of her eyes and she'd lost her teeth a long time ago. Luckily she didn't accept his offer of revenge because the old man was just running his mouth, no way in hell would he have been able to beat up an entire police station with prisoners and everything.'

I remember, with the disbelief that remembering ex-lovers always stirs up, that Jonas's dick was like a magnet for me. My body was pulled to it like a compass, like rain is pulled to the ground. Kevin appeared again, crying because he'd dropped his Coca-Cola. We went to buy another one. 'Kevin's Cleopatra's nephew too. Jessica's son.' 'Great-nephew, then.' They wouldn't have put us in an ad, but the three of us did look like a happy family on the way to the kiosk.

A howl from Cleopatra put a stop to Kevin's crying and the religious chorus. We returned to the heart of the field, to the silence with the kneeling figure of Cleo at its epicentre, her torso rising from the mud with her arms spread wide, in the midst of a dialogue with the beyond. Those of us watching, of course, could only hear her side of it.

'What? What did you say, Holy Mother?'

' . . . . ,'

'No, I don't understand thou. We should grow something? What could we grow, and where? We don't have much land here, unless we move, of course. Please explain, Mother of God.'

'. . . . .
. . . .
. . . .
. . . .
. . . .,'

'But we don't have water either, for Christ's sake!'

'. . . . .
. . . .?'

'Sorry, please forgive me, kind and forgiving defeater of the serpent, I'm going to shut up now, I swear to thou.'

'. . . . .?'

'Oh, no, I will not take the Lord's name in vain again, please speak to me, mother of mine.'

'. . . . .
. . . .
. . . .
. . . .
. . . .
. . . .
. . . .?'

'Yes, I think I understand, oh divine genius. Fish. Of course.'

'. . . . . ,'

'Right, fish in El Poso. We'll become fishermen, like the apostles, mother of mine?'

'. . . . .
. . . .?'

'I will be thou's female Peter, I will carry the weight of your church on my back. May the Lord be with you, Mary, full of grace, our Lord is with thee...'

And blessed art thou among women, everyone started praying again as their curiosity was displaced by the fear that the Virgin would get angry or Cleo would get angry and the huge weight of the hopes that the voices had raised on high that morning would be dashed. There was something sacred in the moment.

'I thank thee, Mother, but how do we go about doing that?'

'. . . . .'

'Oh… yes, of course, you're right, I'm such a moron, sorry, I mean a silly billy, we have to call an engineer. Thank you, dear Virgin, you're so kind to us and you always think of everything!'

We all went quiet, even me – I'd finally joined in with the collective curiosity – until a new howl broke the silence once again. There's no two ways about it: faith, when it's deep, is also very loud.

'Oh! Oh! Oh! I can't believe it! God exists! Look at my legs!'

The wheelchair looked electrified: Susana Giménez was kicking wildly, and laughing hysterically and shouting 'I'm going to walk! I'm going to walk down the marble stairs again! Thank you, dear Virgin, thank you Cleo, my darrrrling!'

10. CLEO: 'THE WATER STARTED
TO FLOW'

The water started to flow that day, and oh, my love, we really turned the slum into a little Venice! It was so beautiful! But that was later and I want to be organised and not branch off like you. More than telling a story it seems like you're telling a tree. You always branch off, Quity, and you skip over bits too. The only thing that matters here is that the story began when the Virgin told me we had to farm fish like the Apostles. And Susana, what a diva! The Virgin performed the miracle on her and she immediately made all the headlines. She shrieked like a madwoman, like some kind of geriatric Barbie ambulance, interrupting my dialogue with the Heavenly Mother. I remember I was furious about her screaming as she left but Ernestito, whom I baptised myself, 'as of today your name will be Rooster and with your red Mohawk you're going to protect the henhouse', told me that as she left Susy had sworn she was going to put me on TV.

I forgot about everything and the little girl inside me jumped for joy. Everyone was watching me in silence and then Ernestito, or Rooster, asked me again, 'So?' And I said: 'I'm going to be a star, Rooster my darling!' And I smiled with all my teeth like I smile now, although now I smile better because of my bright white implants. And it was

Gladys, Ginger, who said: 'No, you idiot, we want to know what the Virgin said.' So I started babbling, saying we had to do it exactly like the Virgin said, not just any old how. She said we should use the field for aquaculture, which is like agriculture but with fish. People have been doing it for ages, like 500 years before the Virgin was born, like 485 years before she had Jesus. And don't go thinking that just because she was a virgin she had it easy, her labour was as painful as anyone else's. She says it was like shitting out a watermelon. Poor thing, she's so good she shouldn't have to suffer, but the Bible says she did, doesn't it? And everything happened just like it was written, she said. She gave me a Bible to read. It's bloody long. I asked if she could get the information into my head some other way since she works so many miracles all over the place. But no, apparently she can't. She says we have to work so that God sees our effort and rewards us for it. I remember shouting: 'I haven't even started yet and he's already rewarding me. I'm going to be on TV! They say it makes you look fat, I wonder if I'll look like a whale.' The whale thing reminded Ginger about the fish, so she interrupted me: 'Cleo, what about the aquaculture?' And her husband, Ernestito, who'd taken the whole thing about being the Rooster very seriously and wanted to restore order, added: 'Get a hold of yourself, Cleo, we want to hear about the thing with the fish.' I remember I got angry then and swore at them. I said something like, 'You lot can be such selfish arseholes sometimes but I love you anyway. The aquaculture thing is like planting fish. Don't look at me like that! You put the fish in the water, throw them food and they reproduce. What we have to do is dig a pond here in the field. Turns out the reason it floods is because the dirt's full of clay. It's nothing but mud, see? And that means it'll keep the water in. So we can dig down and we'll hit water. It's already there, underground. If you don't believe me, go and ask the rich ladies in the neighbourhood who had to move their brats' playrooms out of their basements because the water got in. The Virgin said they prayed and prayed, asking her not to let them flood anymore. And then Mrs Alagarqueta chimed in. Remember that old lady, Quity? She backed me up: 'You're absolutely right, dear, a disaster; the water ruined a billiard table my husband's great-great-great-grandfather, Marcelo T. Alvear, brought over two hundred years ago from Paris. Luckily the sword of my great-great-great-grandfather, Justo José de Urquiza, the sword he used in that famous battle to defeat the tyrant, was in my office. If it had been ruined, I'd have just died! It's a relic of Argentine heroism! A piece of history! So you see, you're not the only ones who suffer from the floods, the water affects everyone equally. My husband owns a construction company, he's an engineer. If I tell him it's something for the Virgin, I'm sure he'll help us build the pond. What kind of fish do we have to grow, dear?'

'My dear', I replied, 'it's true the water floods everyone, but you have to realise that it's not the same to lose your grandfather's table to the water as it is to lose your grandfather himself. They're different categories of antique, you understand?' She gave me a sympathetic look that said she understood there was a difference, so I continued: 'She says we should grow the ones like they have in the Japanese Gardens, what are they called? Arp? Parc? Carp! Oh yes, they're beautiful! All orange and red with white spots, I think, but I don't really remember. Do you remember, Ernestito? When we were little boys we'd jump over the wall into the park and feed them. They'll eat any crap you give them. We just threw whatever we had with us, hotdogs, chorizo sandwiches, and they ate it up, *chimichurri* sauce and all. And if you put your hands in the water they try to eat your fingers.' 'Of course I remember, Cleo, but why carp? Is that what the Virgin said?' Ernestito asked. 'You guys are such a pain in the arse. How should I know why it has to be carp? They're pretty fish, what the hell. Or would you rather raise dolphins here in the field? The Virgin said carp, not sharks or whales, so stop wasting my time. You can't go questioning every word that comes out of the Holy Mother's mouth.'

11. QUITY: 'ON THIS LAND SO FERTILE'

> *On this land so fertile*
> *this pampa so unique*
> *we dug down deep*
> *and up sprang a creek:*
> *stronger than the hose of the fireman*
> *more soothing than the gas of the dental technician*
> *clear, clean and mineral-laden*
> *miraculous, refreshin'*
> *like the waves of the Jordan.*

The stream burst through the guts of the earth, cracking the layers of bones, roots, corpses and worms, and a whole confetti of rubbish, both ancient and contemporary, filled the air. The stream spread over itself to form a pond and the historical debris floated on the surface for a few days: two cannons, a washtub, a newspaper, a pot, a gold bejewelled cross and a barrel of oil. That this had all been part of what Liniers brought with him from Uruguay to fight the English we found out later when the archaeologists came from the university with long ladders and managed to snatch from the stream what they claimed was theirs. Curiously, they said, they only found things from the beginning of the nineteenth century, the end of the twentieth and the beginning of the twenty-first, as if for two hundred years no one had settled there, or as if the shantytown had been built across a street like a kind of permanent picket line. It was evident from the materials used to build the houses that the slum was fairly modern, some people said, to which Cleo sensibly objected, telling them not to be idiots, that the materials were always more or less new because every now and then a storm would wash everything away. Slums weren't built with the same things as the Taj Majal. Where the hell had they ever seen the ruins of the slums of the Roman Empire? Slums rot, burn and blow away, like when Lady Berretguy from the posh neighbourhood nearby was decapitated by a strip of sheet metal that blew off a shack and landed right in the middle of her greenhouse, the only part of her mansion that didn't have bulletproof glass. The rest of the stuff the wind carried off that day was blown into the gardens of the other mansions and the owners donated everything to a charity run by the church, which in turn caused a chaos of biblical proportions because the church handed everything out to the people in the slum without worrying who'd been the original owner. This, of course, started so many arguments between the people and the clergy that now whenever there's a storm they close the doors to the chapel, put the bells into storage and go and watch TV.

The cannons that were dug up had as many inscriptions on them as there are scratched into the rocks of Mar del Plata: 'Royal Spanish Armada', 'English Buffoons', 'Long Live the King', 'Realist to the Bone But Never a Naturalist', 'Get Out Napoleon', 'The Soldier Who Flees Lives to Fight Another Battle'; all easily legible to the naked eye. The kids from the archaeology department came stomping in to take everything they thought belonged to them. Of course they immediately got stuck in the bottomless mud that served as the base of the pond and all we had to do was surround them and stare at them to let them know that anything they found there was not theirs but ours. They came back the next day and set up an office where they could study our relics in situ; no self-respecting group of students would want the authorities to forcibly remove the items on their behalf. The stream never stopped flowing, and they say that even today it's wearing away the foundations of the fancy gated community the tycoon known as El Jefe built there. All we did was contain the flow with walls and make a drain that connected to the nearest gutter. 'One lot of water washes the other and they both go down the gutter,' said John-John, who helped us on his time off from his job as a cop, repentant as he was of his previous sins. 'You have no idea, man, the girls I fucked, but God punished me because screwing girls who don't want you to is a violation of the human rights they teach us in the academy.' 'Yes, John-John, raping people is bad.' 'And my little bird stopped singing and died. He was mute for ten years until Cleopatra forgave me, and then he turned into a finch! He turned into a penguin! Wait, do penguins sing? Are penguins real? My wife's expecting now, and we're going to name him Diego María, Diego after Maradona – it was his birthday the day Jénifer Teolinda told me she was pregnant – and María after the Virgin Mary.' 'And what if it's a girl?' 'Then we'll name her María Dieguina,' said John-John, and he laughed, showing all the fake teeth he'd paid for in instalments through Blue Blood Health Insurance. Poor John-John, ever since he started believing in the Virgin he'd stopped accepting illegal side jobs. 'No way, José,' he'd say from time to time. 'You can't get rich as a police officer without violating the laws of God. The salary they give you isn't enough to live on legally, but I won't go around raping people any more. Not that I can honestly say anyone ever paid me to do that.' And then he'd cover his dick with his hands, as if to protect it from temptations and punishments.

We added a new committee to all the ones we already had; the Transvestite Committee, the Paraguayans, the Thieves, the Peruvians, the Evangelicals, the Bolivians, the Ukrainians, the Buenos Aires locals, the Catholics, the Prostitutes, the Northerners, the Umbanda Worshippers, the Cardboard Collectors and all the other possible combinations. The Historical Committee was in charge of working with the archaeologists, who were happy to be able to teach their science to the community, and the community was happy to learn something other than a technical skill so poorly taught that it wouldn't even have landed Theseus a job. All those courses in sewing or computing, knitting, healthy eating and whatever other bullshit the ruling class seem to think people in the slum need in order to better themselves. The archaeology work was a whirlwind of digging, covering and dividing the site into perfect squares with string. Then the artefacts from all time periods began to appear, most of all bones, the bones of dead people of course. 'This must be why the pampa is so infinitely fertile,' said Daniel, to which Jonas replied, 'Yeah, like Chico Trujillo's song "Harvesting women", and he walked away singing. Daniel laughed and said, 'Your boyfriend's a moron.' And I said, 'Yeah, theoretical speculation isn't his strong suit.' And as we chatted we put the bones into bags, wearing gloves and using little brushes to clean them off first. We sang sometimes and played at being forensic anthropologists, who in fact also came to see the site and found it fascinating. We had dead bodies that were both foreign and domestic, dead of every colour, dead bodies mutilated in the last dictatorship, dead Armenians from the genocide no one remembers, dead victims of starvation during the last democratic governments, dead Africans from Rwanda, dead Russians from the revolution in St Petersburg, dead Communists from all the revolutions everywhere – we even found one of Spartacus's teeth – and dead Unitarians from the civil wars with corn cobs up their arses, and dead natives with no ears (there were a tonne of those, more than anything else). 'They're the roots that wove the world's breadbasket,' I said, and the anthropologists laughed. 'But they're pretty dry now, aren't they? We don't even have any roots left.' When we connected the pond's drain to the storm gutter several of the dead were washed out to sea. For all we know, they've made it back to their homelands by now, or even emigrated. Maybe that's how the dead travel.

Cleo took up a new cause: 'I'm sick of stepping in piles of shit, there isn't a pair of shoes that can survive this mud full of shit. They all get ruined, even the best ones. Look at the designer pair Susana gave me, I wore them twice and the third time a green turd took a bite out of them. I'm serious. I don't know what happened but it looked like a tiger had chomped on them, and even worse, the kids put everything in their mouths so it's like they're born sucking on shit.' Then she proposed a solution: 'Why don't we install pipes and pump it all to the other side of the wall? I asked the Virgin and she said it was a good idea, that it wasn't hygienic to live like this and she'd only seen a situation this bad once, in Avignon, when the papacy was there, she said, and even that idiot Petrarch complained about the shit. Do you know who that idiot Petrarch was, Dani?'

'Yes,' Daniel answered, and he started reciting: 'Laura, with her snowy face and golden hair / whose love has never failed or deceived / in all the history of the world / the way was never so open to a mortal man / to achieve, as you can, immortal fame'.

'Golden hair? Immortal fame? Did he write that for Evita?'

'No, for Laura, that idiot Petrarch was in love with some girl called Laura.'

'Oh, so he was a romantic! Do you reckon the Virgin thinks romantics are idiots?'

Daniel and Cleopatra could go on like this for hours. They always found something to talk about.

12. CLEO: 'I KNOW'

I know how you met: Daniel told me, doll. It's like you think you were the only one who had other lovers before. I had them too: Father Julio and Daniel. Yes, Quity, I already know what you're going to say, that of course the church and the cops wanted to fuck me. And they did fuck me, but I didn't give it away for free. Oh, I don't know why but as I'm recording this it's like I can hear what you'd say if you were here and I was talking to you for real. You get so upset over every little thing, my sweetness. It's like you didn't know that before the Virgin I was a hooker. How else do you think we trannies make a living, love? You think we just show up for a secretary job advertised in the paper and they say 'Welcome aboard, madam!'? Did you ever see a queen working in an office? The one who liked getting sucked off by Ginger was El Jefe Juárez, the guy Daniel killed, my dearest darling, and you watched it all, and since you didn't do anything to stop him, Quity, it's like you killed him too. I pray day and night for the Virgin to ask God to forgive you, but she says God doesn't like people who take justice into their own hands even though she can understand it sometimes if it's done in God's name, but you didn't kill El Jefe in God's name, you killed him in your name, Quity. That's what the Holy Mother says, and I think I'll have to pray to her till I'm eighty. I know you didn't pull the trigger with your own hands, but you knew Daniel was going to kill him and you didn't say anything. I would've convinced him to come here and not to kill that bastard Juárez at all. But you, no, you didn't say a word because you thought it would be better for your book if someone killed that piece of shit. Because you don't have much imagination, you need things to happen for real to be able to write about them.

So I find myself having to pray to the Virgin every day for you as well and she doesn't want to hear it. And don't start bitching when you hear what I'm about to say: I'm her mother too and I have the right to share my faith with my daughter, you understand? If our girl believes in God so much it's because she spends all her time with me and you don't pay any attention to her. But anyway, little Cleopatra also prays for you and talks to the Virgin, who loves children by the way, not for nothing is she the mother of humanity and of Jesus too. He said it himself, 'Let the children come in me'. Isn't that what he said? Or 'come to me'? I think Father Julio taught it wrong. But, ok, we were talking about Dani. I know something you don't. Put this down, but put it down exactly the way I'm saying it. He saved you the day you killed the girl that was burnt by the Beast, that colossal bastard, El Jefe's employee of the century. I don't know why he saved you. He knew you, he was fond of you. Apparently you look like Diana, his daughter. He gave me the picture he took of you that night, honey pie. It's the one I carry in my wallet along with the one of little Cleopatra. That thing you call an ink stain is your aura, because even though you're a nonbeliever, you have a good soul in the photo.

He was there, back in the slum, taking pictures of auras and hoping to find a new messiah or I don't know what. He's not a good soul but he wanted to find good souls anyway. I think he wants to be a bouncer at the gates of heaven or something like that, and it seems he couldn't find any good souls in that gated community in Quilmes where he had his mansion. Did you see the house that crazy motherfucker had? It was gorgeous, everything shone, even the kitchen towels gave off, like, a white light. Daniel said: 'Everything's clean except my soul.' I think he was looking for an excuse for having such a dark soul. 'I can't have a bright soul if someone's killed my daughter.' He was convinced of it, he told me one day, sobbing. He wanted to be part of Christ's army but he couldn't because he wasn't really a believer. He said to me sometimes: 'I'm a crusader with no faith.' And yeah, you're right when you say a crusader's a butcher with or without faith, Quity, but without faith it's even worse.

I don't know what the hell Daniel liked about the slum. I don't know what you liked about it either but I have my suspicions: for you, we were like the geese that laid the golden eggs, but not for Daniel. He wasn't interested in money and much less in fame. He went around everywhere with that little camera of his, looking for good souls for some reason or other. Dani said the biggest soul he'd even seen was mine and then yours was the second, that after you gave that girl the mercy shot you were bursting with light like a comet but he never saw you shine like that again. He said that with Jonas nearby your soul got pinkish, my love. He never took a picture with me inside you, but if he had he'd have seen you looking red like a hot iron rather than pink. How shameless you are, you little devil. If only he knew.

Oh, sorry, my mobile's ringing, I'm turning it off, it rings so much it sounds like an alarm. Ok, it's off now, I'll keep on dictating for you, Quity. And you'd better transcribe me right, because I'm going to read what you put down.

The thing is that Dani got to the scene right after it happened and he saw you running away on the screen of his Kirlian camera. He pulled out his cop badge, stopped the Beast's guys and told them: 'Search over there. Her pimp set fire to her.' *Crónica TV* was already filming and the Beast's guys didn't understand why Dani had done them the favour, but since no one was accusing them of burning the girl they decided to play along and pretend they were there working the case. By the time the cops arrived they were already the heroes of the week, the girl's body wasn't even smoking any more and you were back home and fast asleep, I'm sure of it. I know you. You must have been out like an ostrich after a handful of those pills you take when you can't handle the pressure. That's why he left you a thousand messages, he wanted to know how you were. And to cheer you up he offered to let you watch all the videos no one's allowed to watch except them and even though you have no curiosity and you don't give a crap about anything. When you finally saw me, your ambition got the better of you. You thought you had the story of the year when he told you about me, and you know and I know that's what you liked about us at first. And I'm not even sure you ever liked anything else. I mean, yeah, I know, you fell in love with me too. You do love me, in your way. And in the end you got the best story, the best chick and the biggest dick in the whole of greater Buenos Aires. All in one, my sweet little birdie.

13. QUITY: 'WHAT WE HAD IN
THE SLUM IS LOST'

What we had in the slum is lost. Yes, just like paradise is lost and lost are its meadows and the shade of its trees and the branches bent from the weight of flowers and fruits that shone like gems and birds that sang like angels. And the rushing rivers that never flooded or quenched anyone's thirst because no one was thirsty, the hungerless beasts who lived in peace, the sexless couple and the mild clime. And those trees, the tree of good and the tree of evil and the tree of life. Many trees remain in the world, that's a fact, but there are no more like those. In the slums in particular there were no trees of any kind. El Poso was no exception. We did plant some. We transplanted some to be precise, but not even the dozens of ficus trees and the thousands of cans of geraniums and impatiens with which we bordered the pond could transform it into a *locus amoenus*. The only similarity to the Garden of Eden was the proximity to the divine; the Virgin has a bit of goddess in her even if she's not part of the Holy Trinity and much younger than Jehovah.

Now, maybe, the slum looks a little more like paradise than it did then, but only because it used to be full of so much loss and longing. Sometimes, these days, drunk on martinis and the Caribbean view, we try to plan a new slum, to imagine how we'd recreate what we've had and lost.

There are plenty of raw materials: slums, slums and more slums. If you want proof, all you have to do is follow the curves of wealth distribution in Argentina.

And if the graphs aren't proof enough, Cleo says the Virgin tells her there are more and more slums in Buenos Aires, and they're still about as similar to the Garden of Eden as monkeys are to rocket ships that take tourists to the moon.

We were missing trees, God, lions nursing lambs, armies of killer cupids and a spinning sword. The differences lay not only in what we were lacking; what we had too much of also failed to resemble Adam and Eve's country club. No one expects any Eden to smell like shit, to cite just one of the abundances that ruined the comparison. Because the smell of shit isn't just a nasty smell. The smell of shit is the smell of decomposition, of death in progress.

And it's not that I expected, like Dante, an 'eternal pearl to accept us into it, as water accepts a ray of light, though still, itself, unbroken'. Beatrice, what a strange Beatrice Cleo turned out to be for me. But what an even stranger Dante I am for her. You see, I wasn't expecting anything, not an eternal pearl, not a goddamn thing, but we did have some pretty flowers in the slum. They weren't eternal, it was a miracle if they even lived for fifteen days and we spent all our time harassing gardeners to give us impatiens and petunias and primroses and tulips. Yes, tulips: a kind of Dutch delirium would overcome my woman from time to time. I wasn't on the Decoration Committee but I know they'd go out every week looking for plants because I was the head of the Institutional Relations Committee for the whole time our paradise lasted. And I spent all my time trying to appease everyone who came to complain, angry as hell that the kids from the slum were constantly threatening them. That's how I met Wan. Later on he went back to China and opened an Argentinean supermarket, the clever bastard. He sells pumpkins and *yerba mate* and whatever the hell he tries to pass off as Argentine beef and wine and French bread, all at astronomical prices. In Beijing, Wan even sells *choripanes*, or chorizo sandwiches as he may have to call them. Yes, the modern Chinese man loves luxurious consumption.

We'll get back to Wan later, but first I want to finish: the slum, not even now there are no sheet metal shacks left, now it's all as long gone as Kevin, still doesn't look like paradise. But the strange thing is that it did look a little like paradise before. There was something sacred there and it wasn't the Virgin. Well, it was the Virgin too.

Everything flourished. El Poso looked like Amsterdam with all that water and so many flowers and so much marijuana smoke, but nothing flourished as well as the carp in our world, which, I repeat, was nothing like the world in the Bible. Up there beside God, between the Tigris and the Euphrates, do people sleep together? We already know they do on Olympus, and that perfumed meadows grow wherever Zeus and Hera have gone at it. In the heaven for Muslims I imagine they do too. If not, why would they promise seventy virgins to every warrior who dies for Allah? To serve them *mate?* I doubt it. Cleo, could you ask the Virgin what the dead Arabs want with so many girls? She must know, they're her neighbours.

We slept together too, of course, not to reproduce, but, as anyone does when there's abundance, we devoted ourselves almost exclusively to pleasure. And to eating carp stew, carp with *chimichurri* sauce, carp chop suey, carp soup, sweet and sour carp, carp salad, carp with sautéed vegetables, carp with polenta, carp ceviche and, of course, grilled carp. Ginger, Dani, Rooster and Cleo spent two days shut away with Wan learning all the recipes. Two whole days inside Hermosura, our Chinese friend's supermarket a couple of blocks from the main entrance to El Poso. It was a shitty old warehouse where he sold single cigarettes and watery coffee and noodles and rice and boxes of wine and blonde hair dye, because the women in the slums want to be blonde just like women almost everywhere else. Hermosura also had music: it was always blasting out horrible melodies, a kind of Chinese evangelical *feng shui* that our Taiwanese friend enjoyed immensely. He spent hours at the till, humming, putting away the cash and smiling at everyone. 'It's hard to be a foreigner,' he explained later. And now we know he wasn't lying.

Two women from El Poso who worked at the supermarket told Wan about our aquaculture initiative. Wan loved the idea and dedicated himself to the project as if it were his own. I won't go into too much detail, but 'Papa Wan carp Taiwan' joined the troops of El Poso. He showed up every day with his seven kids to feed the carp we'd managed to steal from the Japanese Gardens. He didn't even care that the shantytown, as well as providing him with cheap labour, bred the kids who robbed him from time to time. He just greeted them with an 'I know you, no rob Wan no more' when he passed them in the alleyways of the slum. Who knows, maybe he thought the work the mothers did for him made up for the damage caused by their kids, or maybe he was just hoping he could finally convince them to leave him alone. And eventually they did leave him alone. As he himself used to say, 'I Chinese, not idiot.'

He must have left Argentina for the same reasons we did: a mix of fear and disgust and the desire to go on living. Or maybe the Virgin ordered him to leave too, as my beloved claims she ordered us to, even though Wan didn't believe in the Holy Mother. He was happy in Argentina: 'China tax children,' he said. 'Many people there, all pile together. Here more better.'

Rooster, Daniel, Ginger, Cleo, Wan, Helena, Torito and

I all used to go to the Japanese Gardens. To be accurate: the ones that reproduced the most were the carp, yes, but the ones that screwed the most were Helena and Torito. I don't know why they came along that night: all they did was start doing it on top of a little bamboo bridge and then fall in the water, and after that they couldn't stop laughing. It wasn't hard to catch the carp, anyway. Although Ginger might not agree with that: she had to seduce a couple of security guards. 'I can take care of both of them in fifteen minutes, so hurry up because it's pretty disgusting to have to jerk off these two pigs,' she said quietly as she took an officer's dick in each hand. It was the special midnight entrance fee to the gardens.

Cleopatra started to pray to the Virgin for forgiveness, 'because it's not good to steal, and it's even worse to suck off security guards'. Wan, who almost never had much to say, considered it necessary to clarify: 'Me, Jesus, Virgin, no believe,' and Cleo interrupted her communication with the Holy Mother to shoot him a furious glare. We intervened and reminded everyone convincingly that God is love, that differences don't matter and one should love thy neighbour. Cleo went back to praying and Wan went back to selecting the carp that were 'more good, more eggs, more babies'. He must have chosen well: we carried away about twenty fat carp of every colour in plastic bags filled with water. That was in November and by March we had 1,200 of them.

14. QUITY: 'LONG LIVE THE SLUM VIRGIN'

Long live the Slum Virgin
may her party never end
there's always room for another friend
here where there's so much blow and beer
that it's coming out of our ears.

She was reflected in the murky water of the pond, looking down with her hands outstretched, always ready to provide refuge. Sometimes, when it rained, the kids tied a plastic tarp to her arms and set up a tent. All children, no matter how poor or criminal, love to play.

Like a slum Narcissus dressed as an Andean god, the Virgin of El Poso watched over the murky pond day and night. And day and night the carp broke the reflection with their whites, oranges and reds. And browns too, from the mud their voracious restlessness stirred up. The people in the slum took care of the Virgin. They put a raincoat on her when it rained, sweaters when it was cold. What would the Holy Mother think of her scarecrow effigy?

For Christmas they twisted lights into her golden rays. I found out later that the rays symbolised virginity. Why rays, Cleo? I asked. Did the sun shine out of the Holy Mother's private parts or something?

And she wasn't the only one who watched the pond. The entire shantytown watched it. The usual chaos was exchanged for order as if the years of poverty and precarity, the narrow alleys covered in shit, the strips of sheet metal, the bricks of different sizes and colours, the crooked walls and the frenzied children had all been caused by the lack of a pond. As soon as we'd filled it, everything began to seem like part of a plan, something with meaning and purpose. As if this miserable labyrinth had been part of a grand scheme, poverty began to feel like austerity, an aesthetic choice.

'The pond's like a miniature version of the shantytown,' said Daniel. Cleopatra thought so too and crowned the barrier wall with another Virgin. One rectangle enclosed the other and both were protected by a Holy Mother. The kids played safely between those two mothers. They wanted to pump the water, keep a lookout, feed the fish and organise the harvests. They saw themselves in the mirror of the pond and they stayed, even though they could sense something terrible on the horizon. Because they'd met the fierce hunters who prowled that land and they knew that we too would have nets thrown over us. But they stayed anyway, between the two virgins, ready to fight.

The carp-butchering community had begun to enjoy life, making regular TV appearances when reporters came to cover our aquaculture venture, sleeping with the university girls who came because we were a good case study for their academic papers; the shantytown guys were suddenly heroes. They felt joy. It may not seem like much but there's little more you could ask for. The saints stayed too. We cemented them to the top of the wall so the Virgin wouldn't be all alone up there, and so 'they can watch over us forever', as Rooster said, laughing as he crossed himself and slathered cement onto the holy feet. Forty saints of varying kinds of saintliness looked down on us, in addition to the police and

TV cameras that also looked down on us, and they all saw themselves reflected in the water of the pond.

The saints had their backs to the motorway, rising up behind the adverts that, of course, faced the passing cars. The mayor, Baltasar Postura, exploited the advertising potential of every last inch of wall. It felt good to have the saints up there like dwarves keeping a lookout over the shantytown. The people outside could keep their fancy saints, sculpted from marble and wood and plaster.

The people outside, the ones who saw the backs of our cement saints' heads, the ones who went to cathedrals, who saw their reflections in the roadside ads just like we all saw our reflections in the pond, began to talk about 'the shantytown saints' and 'the Slum Cathedral'. Whenever I saw Evita's bun-wearing effigy on the walls of the shacks, I wondered what she'd do if she were alive. Would she invite Cleo to work with her elbow to elbow at her charitable foundation? Would she shower us with gifts? Would she take Torito to live with her in the Presidential Palace? Would she come and throw stones into the gardens of the mansions that were separated from the slum by a simple wall and thousands of dollars of income per capita? If Evita Perón were alive, we'd all be Peronists.

'And, of course, Che Guevara would approve,' said Daniel every time we saw his bearded effigy tattooed on the biceps of some boy. Everyone wanted to be like Maradona back then, which included copying the footballer's Che Guevara tattoos. Incidentally, the legendary player had at that time just become even more legendary after being caught measuring out a long fat generous line of cocaine with two teenage girls hiding in his wardrobe. 'That old bastard, he must take first-rate blow, around here everyone crashes by the age of thirty,' said Jonas. 'You forget he was an athlete, *mens sanos in cuerpores sanos*,' Cleo answered without thinking. She wanted to convince the kids to do sport; she thought the best salvation would be for them to go and play football instead of smoking that nasty and lethally cheap mix of cocaine base with glue, crushed glass and who knows what else, known as *paco*. She would lecture the kids who actually listened and little by little they began to 'save themselves', as they said, having waded into the semantic field of salvation without realising it.

As greedy and colourful as our fish, we ate together at midday and at night. We all ate, somehow there was always enough for everybody and it was always delicious. 'The multiplication of the loaves and the fishes,' said Daniel with a hint of forbearance as he looked at the never-ending lines of carp spread out over thirty feet of improvised grill. Grilling was our preferred cooking method. The slum gourmets had their secret techniques for barbecuing almost anything, though maybe not cats. We made the fire with things we found in the street: newspaper to light it, and pieces of wood. The savages chopped down any tree they could get at in the neighbourhood, which, as we know, weren't very many. Everybody talked in loud voices sitting at the long table made from planks and sawhorses, turning off the music only when Cleopatra prayed at the edge of the pond, morning and night, between Jesus and his mother. Sometimes, when the partying wasn't too wild, after dinner she'd tell the stories of the Virgin's miracles. 'Listen up, you' – she spoke a mix of lower-class River Plate dialect and proper Cervantes Spanish – 'and hear what the Holy Mother hath done when some demons cooked up a huge shit-show to steal the soul of a pilgrim, pilgrims being the guys who walk to churches that are really far away from them. It only counts if the church is a really bloody long way away.' And she began to tell the story of an epic poem compiled by Alfonso the Wise eight centuries ago. After spending the night having sex with a hooker, the pilgrim happily continued his pilgrimage to Santiago de Compostela without confessing. The Devil, who apparently competes with God to see who can keep the most souls and rakes them in hand over fist, disguised himself as the apostle Santiago and appeared to the pilgrim: 'Thou must save thy soul so that it does not burn eternally in the lake of fire in hell, where it will surely end up without my help, which is why I'm telling thee: eliminate that which has caused thy sin. Cut off thy guilty member.' The pilgrim chopped it off and then bled to death in the road. The demons called it a suicide and rose up in legions to take him down into hell. And then came the moral, since Cleo didn't tell stories just to pass the time: 'Suicide is a sin, get it? You have to die when God so wants it and not whenever you happen to feel like it. And suicide isn't just when you put a bullet in your head on purpose; it's also when you take too many drugs or when you have sex without condoms, you understand?' And then she finished the story: the Virgin intervenes because she knows the pilgrim's been tricked by the Devil into cutting off his dick, and she brings him back to life. But not completely. She lets a pack of dogs eat his cock, so the man doesn't fall victim to temptation again and is no longer at risk of going to hell.

Everyone laughed. People believed in God, but no one in the slum was afraid of hell. We all agreed, life had a new meaning for us all and we loved each other in this happiness that we experienced and that showed on everyone's faces. It was a never-ending party, life was worth living and we were free in those crowded, cheerful days. The kids were happier: the shantytown was filled with people, students, photographers, NGO workers who doled out the tithes of guilt, and anthropologists and journalists. The residents of the slum were invited to universities to talk about their experiences of self-management. They were interviewed as living proof that 'in this country, effort brings rewards' and they were sent to the provinces to consult on projects people had started in other slums. The press began to talk about 'the Argentinian dream' whenever they referred to us.

15. CLEO: 'YOU'RE FORGETTING EVERYTHING, MY LOVE'

You're forgetting everything, my love. I'm going to have to stop to record something every two pages, and we'll never get to the end if you keep this up. I have to tell the whole story: they might've said we were living 'the Argentinian dream' but the Beast's security troops were shooting at us every day. We cheered whenever we counted a hundred shots with no one dead, because they shot at us like we were the metal ducks in the fairs that would stop near the slum sometimes when I was a little boy. I used to imagine, once I became a little girl, that they won a fluffy toy for every poor person they killed. Because that's why they shot at us, why they'd always shot at us, my love: because we were dark-skinned, we were poor, we were fags or tough guys, because they'd fucked us or because they wanted to fuck us but couldn't. Who knows, maybe they were training for war.

The Virgin says they shot at us because they were tempted by Satan and she also says I should've realised we were always at war. But I'm not sure about that. Forgive me, Holy Mother, but Satan tempts us all and we don't all go around shooting people. Well, plenty of people do, you're right, my darling. That's one thing you and the Virgin agree on, she understands you there. So, we cheered when we counted a hundred shots with no one dead, because it was a miracle they'd all missed us, and there you have more proof of the existence of the Holy Mother. There's no way you don't see it, my love. And that's why we were on the front line when we marched to the town hall. Me, because I knew the Virgin Mary would protect me. And the other trannies right beside me because those huge tits nurse Gómez put in for us were like armour. Do you remember Gómez, darling, who did abortions and tits? Those industrial silicone implants gave us enormous hard tits, which looked either too perfect or totally fake. Yeah, I know my fifty-five-year-old tits shouldn't be harder than your thirty-five-year-old ones, but hey, they are. Don't complain, Quity. You could go to the same surgeon as me if you wanted to, and besides, I like your tits the way they are, a little roughed up by motherhood. Because I have to say that while you may be a disaster with little María Cleopatra, and honestly, I don't know what that girl would do without me, you did breastfeed her for a full year. Now you treat her like she's either a doll or a chore, the way you treat objects. You love her because she loves you and needs you but that doesn't make it any easier for you to put up with her. It doesn't matter, though. She has me.

The point is that in the slum everyone celebrated when we didn't die, and if I'm here talking it's because I've had a lot of days to celebrate. The Virgin wants me to keep on living. I can't even keep count of all the times she's saved me, and I can't believe she chose me for the mission of communicating what she has to say. It's so weird that of all people, the Virgin would choose me, someone who's sucked more dicks than an octogenarian geisha. She says we have no idea how hard it was for her to make herself heard as a fifteen-year-old Jewish single mother two thousand years ago. They hadn't even invented the idea of the Yiddishe momme back then! She caused a huge commotion, she was more scandalous back then than I am now. Maybe that's why she chose me, like she could identify with me because they wouldn't let me be heard anywhere either, they just wanted to put it in me or have me put it in them and that was it. But what I was saying was that they shot at us non-stop, and thank God for our hard tits that wouldn't bend – although they would burst, because, oh dear, all shields break sometime, but in the end it didn't matter. Bullets get through even bulletproof vests, my sweetness. How could you skip the part where we called for justice and all the trannies in the slum walked in the front line of the protest when we marched to the town hall to ask, or more like demand, that Baltasar Postura respect our rights?

And we weren't even talking about putting our female names on our ID cards. No one there even had IDs. We were talking about our right to live, whether they called us Guillermo, Jonathan or Ramón. They can call us whatever they want as long as they let us keep pumping blood through our veins, which is where your blood is supposed to stay. That day we demanded that Postura rein in the Beast. We refused to endure any more of the Beast's apocalyptic fits when the girls didn't pay up or his ravings about Jehovah and flesh consumed by fire and his setting the girls on fire and riddling the boys with bullets if they didn't do what he wanted. Plus, he fucked everyone.

The response came quickly: El Jefe Juárez was sick of the Beast because he was causing so much trouble and everyone at the council was already pissed off with the Condor Security Agency. Don't get me wrong, the politicians were still getting their bribes, they were still getting a cut, Quity my darling, but they were making less than before and it wasn't worth it any more. And the next thing we knew the Beast's car had crashed and burst into flames, do you remember? They'd cut the brake hose or something. The Virgin told me Jehovah had said to her that the smell of that flesh consumed by flames had appeased him. Yes, Quity, don't be so surprised: Jehovah is a bit of a beast too.

16. QUITY: 'FLOWERS, FLOWERS!'

'Flowers, flowers! The Virgin has flowers growing out of her hands!' Torito shouted and he dived into the pond, surrounded, I suppose, by a bubble of bright and confused colours made from MDMA crystals, until he got stuck in the mud and began to giggle hysterically. 'The carp,' he laughed, 'the carp suck me off better than anyone,' and he carried on laughing as he stretched out his fingers and it was true, the carp were trying to swallow him with as much fervour as lack of success. It was a time of open mouths: the carp, who made an O and tried to swallow anything that crossed their path; their way of being in the world was trying to eat it. The bones of the dead in the muddy bottom of the pond, the fingers of the living on its airy surface. And the world ate them: there we were with our bellies full of carp, laughing our heads off, without giving too much thought to the fact that one day we'd be devoured too. From their helicopters, the owners of everything must have seen us the way we saw the carp. As things. We were free for a time, like when Toro thought he saw flowers growing out of the Virgin's hands. Not that they weren't killing us then too; every once in a while they brought someone down, the police and the Condors would spray bullets and some kid would get hit. And of course, from time to time, a kid would kill another kid, just because. If we're going to tell the whole story – and

I'm adding this chapter on your suggestion, Cleo – we have to mention that when a lot of these brainless idiots in the slum got high, if they felt like pulling out their guns and killing people, there was no Virgin in the world that could've stopped them from shooting whoever they wanted.

But we were in the time of miracles and we thought the clumsy statue of the Virgin radiated a protective shield. We all thought it, a little, in one way or another. Including me, since every person is the people just like a drop of the sea is the sea, and I believed in the unity of the people. However it happened, our Virgin was performing her miracles all over the place and we believed in her and we were happy. If she'd been one of those virgins who wept blood we'd have thought she was menstruating: we didn't have time for tears. That time came later. Back then we were almost all still living, and we celebrated the persistence of our lives. There was always someone who kept count of the shots, and when they got to a hundred with no human or sacral victims we broke out the cumbia music, the weed and the beer. It didn't take Toro long to think he was floating among daisies that blew 'like a little breeze' from the Virgin's heavenly hands. He had such a fondness for LSD. He managed to get some hits with pictures of the Virgin Mary on them, although the ones he liked best had pictures of the sacred heart. He'd suck down the squares of acid knee-deep in the pond with the same delight with which the carp sucked his fingers. 'God is love,' he'd say. 'God is love.' We'd all laugh. We were all God. Something sacred circulated among us. Maybe you're right, Cleo, my love. Maybe it was the Virgin herself that transmuted into the air we breathed. It's true that we managed to get rid of the smell of shit.

17. QUITY: 'WE WERE THERE JUST LONG ENOUGH'

We were there just long enough for the feeding of the carp to become a ritual. I don't know where they picked up the habit but our aquaculture pond somehow transformed into the Trevi Fountain for the teenage gangs, who never went out to work without first turning their backs to it. They'd grip their rosaries in one hand and with the other they'd throw in a coin to be sure they'd make it back. At the time I was so consumed by all the new words and images in the slum that there was nothing left over. I didn't think anything of it but it became a custom: those kids waving to the fish and the Virgin were the calm spot in our whirlwind; those poor kids who were always going to die. They did it reverently, seriously, even the ones who were braindead from too much *paco* or coming off a three-day bender with no sleep. They concentrated, their deranged little faces went calm, their disjointed muscles relaxed. The desire to go on living and the belief that that piece of cement painted to look like the Madonna could protect them were the only things strong enough to soothe those masses of nerves, emotions and random thoughts. Seen individually, outside the gangs of dark-headed thugs the media loved to portray, they were beautiful in their fury, a bit like Achilles after his friend dies, when he gives himself over to his rage, to his destiny. Ah, the thieving fury of those teenage thieves...

Cleo was used to it. She's one of them after all, and far from being moved, she used to have a go at them: 'Listen to me, you little morons, are you trying to kill all our carp with your dirty coins? Can't you think of anything better to do with your change?' They could. They started going to the Japanese Gardens to buy fish food pellets. Their presence caused alarm among the Japanese community, who would raise their eyes from their delicate cups of tea, throw down their chopsticks and put on their shoes every time that band of skinny teenagers, whose shoes and weapons were too big for them, showed up in their park. They must've looked like Mishima's child army dressed in their parents' clothes.

Helena Klein met Torito when he had to do some work for the cops. I should explain here that when the police make one of their special deals and promise not to act on somebody's turf, everyone has to pitch in, robbing, thieving and then giving the cops their cut. The police captain himself took attendance. And then off they all went, never failing to pass by the pond first to throw food over their shoulders to the fish behind them and ask the Virgin in front of them for protection so they wouldn't be the ones who were lost that night. Because some were always going die. The cops had to pretend they were doing their job in order to keep their legal salary coming. The kids were allowed to keep thirty per cent of whatever they brought in, but they had to take care of their own funeral expenses. Here in Miami, I have the best teas from around the world and real china teapots. I've become a collector. My daughter doesn't understand why I won't let her play with them, she can't understand that my little selfish pleasures are what keep me together. Her fury and joy keep her together. That little girl's already a confident woman. She owes her happiness and confidence to her other mother, crazy Cleopatra, who still talks to the

Virgin, but now from the beaches of Key Biscayne.

Helena, the redhead, turned up holding Torito's hand after one of those nights. Torito had tried to rob her but he hadn't been able to. She fell in love 'at first sight' and said to him: 'What the hell do you think you're doing?' He explained he had to make money for the cops, and so together they stole some jewels from her mother. Mrs Alvear was suspicious when she saw her grandmother's earrings on the police captain's wife at church one Sunday, but when the captain saw her staring he told her he'd bought them in the city centre. 'Aren't they pretty?' he said, to which Mrs Alvear replied: 'Yes, they're very pretty and they're also mine.' They raided the shop of some Bolivian jewellers, the captain got a promotion, Mrs Alvear got her earrings back and the Bolivians were deported back to Bolivia. Helena turned up, then, and she told us that she knew about fish, that her father had built her an aquarium when she was five years old and that a little while after that he'd committed suicide. Helena was convinced it was because of her mother and her Catholic family, and she devoted all her time to those fish until she'd created one of the most spectacular private aquariums in all of South America. She's a marine biologist now. 'There are lots of different ways of having a father,' she said, and without any further explanation she gradually ended up staying with us. Her mother, Mrs Alvear, widow of the late Mr Klein, was happy that the girl spent time in the shantytown helping the poor and being protected by the Virgin. Even though she didn't think her daughter put as much distance as she should between herself and *those people* – no doubt due to her youthful idealism, she thought – it was still charity in the end, which all the women in her family had done in one way or another ever since the men had decided to put themselves to use and start making money. And they'd needed the money, too – they had done since before the family had made a name for itself, even before their forefathers had first set foot on the continent. Torito was half-Inca, glossy and brown with a powerful neck like a young animal, hence the nickname, Toro, or Bull. I think his real name was Eusebio and it became another custom, like second nature, to see the redhead, Helena riding him all over the place. 'Pray tell my loving father that Europa has left her native land, seated upon a bull, my ravisher, my sailor, and as I think, my bed-fellow. Please deliver this necklace to my mother.' I remembered the line from the myth of Europa every time I saw her climbing onto Torito, that poor Inca who was transformed into Zeus between the magical legs of his Helena.

Helena works here in Florida now, at a university aquarium bigger than the one she had as a girl. She studies the language of dolphins. ('It's not a real language because they don't tell jokes,' she always clarifies.) She was able to save Toro after the disaster: all she had to do was threaten her family and bribe a judge to get him to Miami, but he was already too screwed up. 'With so many friends dead, life hurts,' he said one Sunday and the following Wednesday we found him colourless and dull with a knife stuck in his throat. Helena married a magnificent biologist whose last name was also Klein, becoming Helena Klein-Klein, and for their honeymoon they went to Israel because, as she put it, she was 'used to having sex behind a wall and surrounded by soldiers'.

It was here in Fort Lauderdale that we composed the poem for Torito. We can reproduce it in its entirety here in the book because it's not part of the cumbia opera. Cleopatra recited it at his funeral, which was sadder than mass on Good Friday:

In all the history of the world
the way was never so open to a mortal man
to achieve, as you can, immortal fame
Immortal fame?
The elegant Evita?
Is this the poet Perón,
the workers' champion number one?
No, that's Petrarch's line and it was written
to the aura, to the laurel
to his Laura in the garden
He sang blue onto the wing
I love you and I will sing
to the beat of the guitar
and we will *rememberear*
a mystery great as Mona Lisa
crooked as the tower of Pisa.
So let us sing it from the rooftops
the story of poor Torito:
He came to us a boy so wee
and stayed to join the family
to live forever in the slum
of orphaned *gauchos* and bums
On the pampa's murderous plains
the children wish and wish in vain
for a mother to adore them
or even a dog to paw them
but the fatherless tots toddle
like orphans of the Trojan War
toddled centuries before
but my problem is, I can't pray
if I've never known my *padre*
Should I tell my mother I have come
to offer prayers to her man?
In the name of the Virgin

the mother of my true origin?
It was another form of destitution
what the *vida loca* had in store
Poor Torito and his friends
from beginning to end
destined to be the sacrificial lamb
yet they only managed to defeat him
in the lovely Florida Keys
The fucking American dream
was certainly the death of him
His throat was slit
and the Latino forensics
of Miami-Dade County
thought it was some psycho plan
from Torito's homeland
The Latino cops had heard it said
that Argentina's national pastime
was the dance of the dead
and we sing it like this:
'Press the blade hard under the ear,
steady with the hand till the throat is clear
It takes away all your pains
as it slices through your veins
and as the blood begins to flow
you'll give them such a fright
as your eyes begin to roll'.
But the police don't understand the reality
that Torito's true killers
were the ones who killed his family
And this new land full of immigrants
gave the blade its final twist
It was the Chileans, the Jews, the Spanish
or the Mexicans, who have a song that goes like this:
'On my return at your request

I'll gift to you an elegant dress
of the very finest ilk
lined with the very reddest silk
And for your neck some crimson jewels
fit for a fine lady or lord
And you'll forever be adorned
by the necklace my sword draws'
And did Torito go to heaven
like Petrarch's lovely Laura?
He went, that's for sure,
but the check-in was a disaster
Because someone slit his neck
to see him slip and slide
        in blood
like a sailor on the deck
Then he was a corpse
Oh fleeting daylight!
Oh fragile nature!
Today the sweet flower is born
and on this very day her path shall end
Everything toward death marches
Every beast under the moon
will end up on the barbecue
Here lies dead the matador
Here lies dead the dear friend
Here the ashy body
like leftovers on a grill
He came home to the slum
with bottles of champagne
and cans of beluga
paid for by the posh ladies of Recoleta
who clung with passion
to his hot animal-like neck
which is now cold and cleft

in the morgue of the local district
Death always comes too soon
and won't pardon anyone
It was the wise Cleopatra who once said
even after Satan was defeated
the Baptist was still dead
along with a whole long list
of the Lord's chosen ones
And we believed that He
would remove from the slums
those who were deserving
who had a purpose worth serving
But the slum kids always say
from the very earliest age:
We, the young
will live a life of fun
but it'll be a short one
We take what fate may hand us,
but not even exile can save us
Our death comes so swiftly
that no one reaches fifty
without being shot, stabbed, raped or beaten
till by the worms we're eaten
till we turn to smoke, dust, shadow, nothin'.

18. QUITY: 'SHE WAS AN EVIL, VILE RAT'

She was an evil, vile rat
She could bite a dead man
and turn him to a pile of rot
And there wasn't enough cocaine
alcohol or Valium
in all the slum
to make me forget the stench of her scum.

Almost all animals are more intimidating when they're facing you than when they have their back turned. The rat from my nightmares was the exception. If you looked her in the eyes she was disgusting, repulsive, foul, but she didn't make your brain reel with fear. Vermin should be trampled the way the Virgin, millennia ago, barefoot, trampled the serpent. Virginity wasn't one of my virtues but being a woman must've been enough, because when I looked down her snout, I was certain I'd be able to trample her into a thin furry film, a piece of carpet, a little leaf that could be carried away by a light breeze.

But terror set in as soon she moved away. What a strange threat, my rat, who broke the mould of perspective as she turned around. When I saw her from behind, she threw me into a cold and viscous vertigo, into freefall, a limitless vulnerability that always led to that other nightmare. I dreamt I'd woken up with a monumental hangover: hammering in my head, nausea, diarrhoea, panic. And what was worse, when I looked around I saw a mountain of dead bodies, their presence as inexplicable as mine. I couldn't remember how I'd got there, I didn't know if I'd be the next body added to the pile but I couldn't move because my legs wouldn't respond or because I'd slip on my own vomit or my own shit.

My rat wore a hooped skirt made of excrement and fossils, and carried a rake of shit and bones sharpened as if to till the ground of the slum with death. How could a rat with a plough made of fossils not be terrifying to someone in El Poso, which is nothing but dirt and mud? She reigned over the kingdom of the cardboard collectors, with her cart made of the flesh and bones of the dead that she had transformed into rotting corpses with a single bite.

That damned cardboard collector followed me in dreams the whole time I stayed in the shantytown. The first time I saw her I was terrified. I woke up, but couldn't move from the cot I was sleeping on in Cleopatra's shack. I lay there still and silent and panicked, hardly breathing as I listened to the deep sound that, I thought, was my rat sharpening her claws against the ever-damp walls of the shantytown's shacks. I thanked the Virgin that the debauchery of the night before had led me to pass out before getting undressed or taking off my boots. Panic, for me, has always brought gods into existence.

Convinced she'd only attack if I let my guard down, I spent many sleepless nights conjuring up the dream rat through the noise of the legions of real rats that jumped and skittered on the sheet metal roofs in an incessant and complex choreography. They started on the roofs, but their dance was performed across various levels. On the ground, the vampiric lovers of leftovers dodged the empty boxes of wine that fell off the tables even when there was no wind.

The tables belonged to the cats: in El Poso's food chain, the pests divided the victuals by height. We were an ecological slum, we recycled almost everything. Even the shit was eaten by the rats, those after-hours crap-eating merry-makers.

The chain started with us, or at least that's what we thought: we drank, ate and fucked more or less like anyone else, maybe a bit more, like anyone would if they suspected the world would soon come to an end. Well, definitely more than most: we were insatiable. It wasn't just the alcohol, because we danced so much it evaporated with our sweat in a rhythmic frenzy, in passions that exorcised all our demons. And I'm not speaking metaphorically. There were dances that expelled devils: people would faint and when they woke up they asked for forgiveness for all their offences. Some nights ended in confessions, generalised wailing, group hugs. Ernestito, for example, started believing in the Virgin's miracles after a huge reggaeton orgy. He danced like he was possessed until he passed out and when he came to, he turned off the music, knelt down in front of Ginger and told her that that was it, that she was done getting paid to suck cocks, that they should plant carrots, that he'd refuse to eat so much as a hamburger bought with her arse or her dick. Or with his. He said the Virgin had appeared to him while he was dancing and that the Virgin didn't want them to make a living exploiting their bodies and that, also, ever since they'd got the carp and we'd begun planting tomatoes and squash, no one in El Poso was going hungry. Ginger said he was right and they both ended up kneeling at the feet of the Virgin in front of the pond and everyone crowded around them, crying as well.

I don't know if it was the jugs, or rather the alcohol we filled the jugs with, or rather the psychoactive drugs those lunatics put into the jugs of alcohol, but anyway, we were forever dropping things and falling over, and it wasn't always just the mystic trance that knocked us down. I've fallen over a few times and none of those times have been caused by a push from divinity. If these parties had happened while I was still working as a journalist, I would've used the vulgar qualifier 'drunks' to describe us. Journalism isn't a profession of subtleties, but by that time I was hardly a journalist any more. During those parties, I became a songwriter. And not the most subtle one, I have to admit.

Mystic, ecstatic or drunk, or whatever we were, we left all kinds of crap in the wake of our dinners. What remained on top of the table was eaten by the cats and the birds, with tense scenes playing out between the two groups. The cats gazed pensively at the birds and the birds stared suspiciously at the cats but they didn't fly away. They wouldn't give up their share of the banquet, not even when they ran the risk of becoming part of the feast themselves. Of course, sometimes the cats moved from mere contemplation to action and, with a swipe or a bite, ripped the fright from the birds' eyes. Our birds were sleepwalkers too, the entire slum was a mess of insomniac animals: the pigeons (*Columba palumbus*), the house sparrows (*Passer domesticus*), the parrots (*Myiopsitta monachus*), the song sparrows (*Zonotrichia pileata*), the red-bellied thrush (*Turdus rufiventris*) and the mourning doves (*Zenaida maculata*). They were a South American infantry, incessant and insomniac. We had plagues of parakeets that chased the rats over the sheet metal roofs and hid in the huge pots of geraniums that Cleo had ordered – on the Virgin's suggestion – to be put on the roofs instead of the bricks and chunks of concrete generally used to hold roofs in place in this kind of so-called architecture. Seen from above, the shantytown was a garden, it was a forest of geraniums with nests and all. Even the *horneros* (*Furnarius rufus*) made homes in the geraniums that sprouted from the roofs of their nests.

What the birds and the cats wouldn't eat, the dogs would. Then the cats would be the ones watching suspiciously and the contemplative ones would be the dogs, and sometimes the tension dissolved into battles that ended with shots being fired. The first neighbour who got sick of not being able to sleep would shoot at the sky to scare the dogs, the cats and the birds. The rats stayed despite it all. The bullets didn't seem to worry them.

It was all biting, chewing, swallowing; we could hear the crunching, guzzling and breaking noises of the world eating the world. Our rats gnawed at whatever was left over, the peel and stones of everything: the potato skins and orange rinds, the carp bones, the greasy wax paper salami wrappings, pizza boxes, fingernail clippings spat out by the anxious shantytowners, the foals birthed by the mares that pulled the cardboard collection carts, the cum spat out by the hookers, the hairs that fell from the large shaven transvestites and everyone's shit. All that was eaten by the slum rats, who were as high as we were thanks to the coke we dropped on the ground or left out on the same Formica tables we used to fornicate on top of.

And the boxes of wine: the rats would suck at the cardboard and then chew it up slowly, just like they did with the used condoms. They ended up drunk, lying on the walls of the pond, looking down, who knows, maybe trying to recognise their own reflections or lamenting the fact they weren't sufficiently amphibian to be able to feast on the colourful carp that spun and twirled there in the water and sometimes popped up above it.

The rats looked at the carp and the carp looked at the rats and everything was frozen in that moment of contemplation, which generally came just before sunrise. The only thing that moved was the reflection of the colourful cement Virgin who presided over the pond with her arms open and welcoming, rocked by the breeze. There were never strong winds in the shantytown. It must have been thanks to the huge barrier wall. Or the Virgin, who knows.

Sometimes, a few of the bigger rats would fall into the pond and end up floating like pestilent balloons. And then the carp, accustomed as they were to food falling from the sky (the sky was us, those of us who were still standing and threw them leftovers when the party had just finished and before we went to bed), abandoned their contemplation but not their patience and ate the rats slowly. The scavengers would wait until the fat ones were good and rotten and then suck at them little by little with their toothless mouths. Cleo didn't like it, but we often left them floating there. The carp seemed jubilant when they ate the putrefied rats, they shone, their colours grew brighter, the pond looked like a garden of mephitic carnivorous flowers.

When the party was over, almost every night, the birds, cats, dogs, and the non-imaginary rats stayed awake and took over the slum. And I snorted coke to keep me awake and safe from my imaginary rat. At midday, I drank whisky to help me sleep at naptime when the threat of nightmares faded in the light of the bright Buenos Aires sun. During the day I knew I wouldn't be devoured by a rat. As soon as the evening set in, the fear returned. During the minute and forty-one seconds it takes the sun to go down after touching the horizon, when the sky is seven shades of blue, the first stars come out and even the parrots shut up, my nightmare began: the rat from my dreams stretched out her terrifying paw at the same time as the night stretched out her dark one. And I began to reason with my panic, telling myself that an imaginary rat couldn't hurt a real woman like me.

How the rest of the rats didn't torment me is a question I can't answer fully even today. I wasn't crazy enough not to understand that although an imaginary rat couldn't possibly make dinner out of me, a whole load of real rats might've been able to. But not even in those days did I have much faith in the masses: 'If the people don't understand the power they'd have if they only joined together, what the hell do a bunch of rats know?' I told myself. But that thought didn't help me get to sleep either. The people at least have an idea of their power, just like the rats have a sense of smell. Anyway, however much as I drank and snorted, I couldn't conceive of an army of rats capable of coordinating tactics and strategies; rather, I thought maybe they could smell, with their sniffing snouts, that in that small room built from stolen bricks, plasterboard, dust mites, mildew and sheet metal there were just a few people and a lot of rats. Watching them disperse, trampling over each other, helped me sleep, although I still held my gun in my hand. Thankfully, it was never necessary to prove whether the rats, when unified, could be beaten.

In my flat the rat threat would have disappeared instantly and I would've never vacillated in my atheism. But in the Baroque misery of the slum, where everything was always above, below, inside or next to everything else, anything was possible. And, inevitably, it was also very entertaining. With everything piled up together, everything fucked everything else, even the horses tied to the cardboard collection carts climbed on top of the horses tied to other carts to screw, their bodies smashing against the carts and cardboard.

Ginger woke me up from my naps with a Mexican-style beer. She'd press the lip of the glass into some salt, flip it over, add some ice cubes, Worcester sauce and a splash of Tabasco, and pour the beer in on top. I liked my *micheladas* around seven, when Cleo's second-in-command would appear with my frosted glass. I'd wake up, take a sip and the gunshots and columns of cumbia rose up: 'Today I'll be out on the street huntin' / a pair of crazy *papis* who are ghostin' / I'm always ready…' Like a ceremony, the beer, spice and salt pulled me from my stupor and the midday whisky hangover. Ginger's verbal diarrhoea made me forget my nightmares, and the gunshots that signalled the start of that night's party got me out of bed.

We hung colourful Christmas lights from the roofs of the shacks for the dances. As soon as they went on everyone showed up, like it was some kind of signal. It was a signal, just like it was a signal if someone missed the party two or three nights in a row. It meant they were either dead or in jail, so we'd check the hospitals and police stations. Jessica would always show up at dinnertime. Despite the fact she lived pumped full of pills, she never failed to fill certain gender roles. She paid almost no attention to Kevin. A kid is too high a price to pay for a shag at sixteen, but she'd serve him a plate during dinner and make sure his clothes stayed relatively clean even though she had no idea who was providing the clothes to her son, my son. I bought them for him, spending a fortune on his pre-school hip-hopper style. Or Wan would bring him clothes. He denied he was the father but he adored Kevin: 'No be Wan son, but look like,' he'd say, and he'd give him velvet Chinese outfits embroidered with dragons which Kevin adored. I imagined him as a teenager, with dragons tattooed on his arms and back.

Rooster bathed and groomed the brood of fourteen kids that he and Ginger looked after. As soon as they'd given up prostitution, they began dedicating their time to taking care of any stray kid that wandered through the slum. There were a lot of them, and Rooster made sure they were always clean with hair combed, the boys with gel, the girls with two pigtails, and the teenage boys with bleached spikes that stood up so straight it looked like they had plaster in them. Because before Rooster was a rentboy he'd been a builder; the two professions share a passion for neat hair and he combined this passion with his skills. All fifteen of them would turn up looking like a poster for some working-class barber shop as Ginger, his partner and the kids' adopted mother, got the jugs ready, one of *michelada* and another of orange juice, which is what the kids in the shantytown drank. Torito and Helena always turned up famished, Toro dressed like a cumbia star and Helena in the ripped French denim she wore for all occasions. They did almost nothing but smoke weed and have sex, which was why they were always so famished. Helena supervised the carp and the pond, but everything was going smoothly so the work took her just a few minutes. Dani also came but not always, because he couldn't stand the long hours Cleopatra liked to spend sitting around the table after dinner. I think he was really in love.

The table was very long. We used one of the walls of the pond, which measured over three hundred feet down one side, as a bench. A load of boards resting on thirty sawhorses held up the most communal of our meals. Ginger and some of the other transvestites, all enthusiastic bartenders, brought out drink after drink. Around the third or fourth round, the bodies began to sway to the degenerate rhythm of the reggaeton: 'I'll give you my cream with the delicious taste / all over your hands and in your face,' we sang. Yes, I sang too. At first I resisted those idiotic lyrics and tried reciting classic songs instead ('Let's dance, dear friends, us three / here under the flowering almond tree; / and anyone as happy as are we, / if they know how to love, / will come to dance / under the flowering almond tree') so as not to lose my vocabulary, but the rhythm of the reggaeton, which when you're drinking and dancing is more like sex than music, gradually won me over and began to invade the old songs: 'Let's suck, dear friends, us three / I'll suck you if you suck me / and if you know the right way to work it / in the club up in Florida / we'll be watching you twerk it.' Around the sixth Fernet and Coke, I'd start singing at the top of my lungs, and according to Cleo that first classic song laced with reggaeton was prophetic: 'Darling, do you realise we're twerking in Florida like you prophesied?' she asked me after the Miami premiere of the cumbia opera.

But that was much later. Back then the music was taking over my body and my lexicon and my mind and what had before seemed so stupid began to multiply in every cell. It wasn't just that it no longer seemed stupid; it was that stupidity had ceased to exist as a criterion by which to measure anything. My flesh liked the degenerate rhythm and I began to become degenerate and I enjoyed the swaying of the grill, the lines of chorizos crammed together as they sizzled, drinking from the pitchers spiked with pills, I began to *reggaetonear*, as Jessica said, to *cumbianchar*, as Torito said, to twerk, as everyone else said, fuelled by the 'bam bam bam / give me a light / tonight's the best night'. The queens shouted when it was time for dessert, and they turned up the cumbia even louder: 'get your hands up / if you want a puff / get crazy, real crazy / dancing crazy front and back,' and we threw our hands up and puffed and got crazy front and back and puffed again and I'd remember the story I was writing that had brought me to the slum in the first place and I'd pull out my dictaphone and start following Cleo around. In turn Cleo would talk nonstop about the Virgin, even when she was leaning against the wall screwing someone, she kept talking to me nonstop. My beloved says we were brought together by 'the miracle of having both stayed alive', but that was later. The seed of love was planted in the slum. She adored the attention and my barrage of questions: the queen was turned on by the microphone in my hand, and I'd ask and ask some more even while she was pounding someone, embedding, or 'encrusting', as she likes to say since she loves jewels, her precious stone, her homo sapphire, into an eager arse. Cleo began to fall in love with my desire for her words and she told me her stories and theories even when she had a dick in each hand or was pushing someone's guts in with her own dick. And no one complained because a spray of Cleo's cum was almost like holy water; after all, in all her trans glory, my wife is the Virgin's chosen one. And I also started to fall under her spell, I was turned on by my subject who interrupted my stream of questions with her leonine roar. When Cleo came I got wet and ended up climbing onto the lubricated cock of some dude, anyone who happened to be passing by. In every house, on every table of the slum, it was sex all around: the drunk girls, the girls baked beyond belief who pressed into each other, tits to tits, messing up their hair, smoking joints when the slow stoner cumbia played: 'dance cumbia *cumbianchero* / the stoner's here / high out of his head / tipping back a beer'.

Around that time of the night my rat would be lying belly up, her hoop-skirt plough around her ankles, twerking on her back and swaying her paws to the rhythm of the cumbia. But she was a monster that couldn't be defeated by any bottle. A bit of blow never failed to fly through the air and land directly on my rat. My nightmare was a true vicious cycle, eternally renewed by everything I took to break it.

19. QUITY: 'THEY TOOK HIM OUT
WITH A GUNSHOT'

They took him out with a gunshot
when he went to get his toy
Poor, cold, alone and rotting
my little dead boy.

'Mammals, Kevin, are the animals that grow inside their mummy.' When Kevin understood something, he'd smile and his whole face would squint. In the afternoons when Wan closed the supermarket for a few hours and came to feed the carp with his legions of offspring in tow, Kevin happily got lost in the crowd of Wan's children. He looked like Wan's son and maybe he was; Jessica, his mum, wasn't quite sure, though she did say 'I think something happened with the chinaman'. Wan didn't think it likely. 'Boy born three months after,' he swore, holding up both palms and then counting three fingers of his right hand, but he never stopped sending Jessica provisions from Hermosura so that Kevin would have enough to eat. Every week he sent rice, cans of tuna, tomatoes, powdered milk and little Chinese toys that sang impossible Chinese songs until their cheap Chinese batteries wore out, which was thankfully pretty quickly. He continued to send bags even after I began to take care of the boy.

Kevin adopted me. That's why I stayed. Jessica was lost: she'd become a groupie, 'milkmaids' they were called, of the Blowheads, a cumbia band that lived up to its name. And Cleopatra, Jessica's aunt and Kevin's great aunt, was lost in the heights of her craziness, talking all day long with Saint Mary and lost to the demands of her divine mission of organising the slum. So Kevin understood and he laughed, looking just like one of Wan's sons, and he hugged me. And I can still feel Kevin's little body, that loving shape, warm and safe as he gripped me, as if I were his home. It's strange, because my body generally doesn't remember things. I don't remember the feel of even the men I enjoyed the most. Not even Jonas or his dick, which had me blinded with love the first few months in the slum, until I lost him to the posh young student chicks who started visiting and he lost me to his aunt, who looked so much like him but much larger and more beautiful. In my mind his body began to meld with Cleopatra's until Jonas disappeared completely, way before he was even dead and a little bit before Cleo and I began to feel this surprising love that continues to surprise us to this day.

Jonas realised before I did; lovers always know. He laughed and told me: 'You're less and less picky. First you sleep with a penniless bastard like me and now you're into some kinky lesbian shit: you want to have sex with a broke trannie motherfucker. And don't think that just because she's a trannic you'll be able to take her. My aunt may look like an elegant lady but she can beat the crap out of you. Before she became famous with the Virgin, she was famous for her anaconda.' I was never sure if he thought it was funny or if he was jealous. I didn't care either. I started loving my beloved later, once the slum was a pile of rubble and all I felt for Jonas was sadness over his death and I hardly remembered anything else. But I can still feel Kevin today. Not even little María Cleopatra could erase him from my memory.

Kevin was with me from the first day I spent in the slum, from that cold November morning full of jasmines which seems so remote now with everyone that's died since then, but which was really just a few years ago. At the start of lunch that day he appeared at my side and somehow, even though he wasn't speaking yet, he asked me to feed him. I understood. I was amused by the silent shine of those little black eyes and I sat him on my lap. A bit later on, after we'd eaten, Kevin rubbed my face with his little hands covered in barbecue grease and mayonnaise and gave me a hug and a kiss.

That's why I say he adopted me, Cleo. Don't get offended, I'm not trying to criticise anyone when I say that Kevin took refuge in me. At least, I don't mean to be critical. I don't know, you were with the Holy Mother all day long. And Kevin and I were all alone. No, it's not a criticism, Cleo, get over it: I wasn't with him when he needed me most. I wasn't able to hug him, keep him warm as the warmth left him, call an ambulance to take him to the hospital and threaten to murder the entire medical staff if they didn't save him, or even just keep him company until the end.

I know I always tell the same story. It's not that I forget I've already told it, it's just that I can't stop remembering the scene. That first meal when Kevin found my gun and started pretending he'd been shot, that he'd been killed by a bullet: he couldn't even talk yet but he was a good actor, he shouted 'Baaaaaaaaang!' and grabbed his chest, walked like he was dizzy, fell to the ground and lay still a few seconds until he couldn't hold his laughter in any longer or resist checking for looks of approval on everyone's faces. I remember his shrill little laugh and then once again his simulated falling, and once again his still body, as if my mind were making a failed attempt to console me, as if it were trying to replace the moment when he really did get shot and died forever with this other playful scene. And it works: it's been a long time since I thought of Kevin's death but that other scene, the one I tell the story of over and over, hurts deep down and makes the beating of my heart become irregular. Something broke inside my heart with Kevin's death and I'm not being metaphorical. Ever since they tore down the slum and murdered my little boy, my heart's been sounding like a broken machine. It lost its rhythm, started making strange noises, decreased in elasticity. Sometimes it contracts and stays that way, aching, clenched like a fist, and I know that I'm going to die in spite of the army of cardiologists we pay for.

I also have pretty memories, but they hurt almost as much as the others. And the death of that piece of shit of El Jefe, knowing that in some way he died as a result of my decision, even if it wasn't my bullet, doesn't lessen my pain.

Why did I let Dani kill him then, Cleo? So he'd die, my love. To get just a little bit of justice. Because it wasn't enough for him to go to prison, and he wouldn't have gone to prison anyway.

But for now I want to keep talking about Kevin, my first home. That boy who made a home for me there in your shack in the slum, in that room you'd built out of drywall, full of little angels, prayer cards and stuffed animals. I think the first day I stayed over at your shack, I actually stayed without meaning to. It was because of Kevin, who turned up in his pyjamas hugging his favourite toy, the doll that looked like a bald chef. I was already pretty drunk and sad. I'd started crying, I don't remember why, maybe I didn't even know at the time, but Kevin saw me, he ran back to the shack and returned with some toilet paper. He started to bandage me, do you remember, Cleo, my darling? He bandaged my whole body, from head to toe, with toilet paper. I looked like a mummy. The boy was so sweet, he was curing me, he didn't leave any part uncovered and when he was done he took me by the hand and put me to bed. He hugged me and started singing something like a lullaby, some kind of cumbia song that sounded sweet sung through his mouth. His little body warmed me up, that same little body that, frozen with death, froze me too and shattered me as if the home he and I had built had been made of some kind of glass, and that home didn't die with him, my love, he built it for me and it's still here with you and little Cleopatra but it's cracked by his death. It's as if you and our daughter, who wasn't even an embryo when all that happened, I know, but it's as if all three of us owed him something, the life he didn't have, as if we were guilty for living on without him.

I'd gone to my flat to get some things that afternoon. He wanted to come with me but I had to go to the bank and stop by the newspaper office to settle either another year of hiatus without pay or the termination of my employment, I wasn't sure which. And I wasn't sure until afterwards, when, two blocks from the newspaper, they called to tell me there was an operation in the slum and I called Daniel, who looked into it and told me that it was true. After that, he picked up some shotguns and took off for the slum, and so did I, like a madwoman.

It was six-thirty in the evening, there was a tonne of traffic, my car was dented but I managed to make it through the impossible chaos and onto the Pan-American Highway in forty minutes. I got all the way to Márquez, where everything was blocked off by the police and their urban assault vehicles and their patrol cars and their kids dressed in combat boots and carrying machine guns. I got out of the car and began to walk under the motorway, hearing gunshots in the distance, and when I got there almost everyone was gone. The bulldozers were already busy and the Virgin had already lost her head and the carp were floating dead on the surface of the pond and all that was left were the cops and their machine guns. I was a journalist and I went in with the other journalists. Some were friends of mine and I asked them to help me find Kevin and I think even a few who weren't friends helped me look too. We were all searching for a beautiful dark-haired little boy who looked Chinese and was around this tall. But we couldn't find him, and I couldn't find Cleo either. I was still searching when Daniel showed up. We stayed there until the next morning searching among the bulldozers but there was nothing, there was no one. I never found him.

Days later we got the copies of the security camera footage and what some of the students from a German university had managed to film for a documentary they were making. We also got the footage from the mobile phones of the kids from the slum. That's when I finally saw my little boy, dying, all alone. He wasn't even able to hug his toy, which was just a few feet away from his body. He died with his arm outstretched toward the bald chef doll, shaking with the convulsions of death.

20. CLEO: 'YOU WEREN'T THERE'

You weren't there, Quity. I was. I have to tell it myself. I'll dictate. Take this down exactly, because I'm telling you how things went. I've been called *loca* more times than I can count, ever since I was a little girl. They call all us fags *locas*, so just imagine what they say about the ones who can talk to the Virgin or some saint or with God himself. They all think we're out of our gourds, they think we're batshit. I don't know why. That's just how it is. I never have time to think too much about anything but I know I'm not crazy, I've never felt crazy despite how you make me look in your book, Quity. I was never really insane until that day you're talking about.

We heard the helicopters before anything else. I wasn't worried, I'd talked to the Virgin just a little bit before and she'd said, 'Take care of thyselves, children of mine,' but I didn't pay much attention. I thought it was just a way of saying goodbye, everyone back in Argentina always says 'take care', just like you'd say 'see you' or 'ciao', instead of saying 'adios' like they say here and like the Virgin usually says, which seems right because the *dios* part of that goodbye has something to do with God.

I didn't pay much attention because I thought she'd look out for us and I wasn't so worried about myself, just about the kids taking drugs or the girls getting stolen and taken to whorehouses and whether everyone was wearing condoms and that was it; I thought she'd take care of the rest. When we heard the helicopters, I was just a tiny bit scared. They'd already called from the court to tell us to vacate the slum. We were going to be moved to a gorgeous new neighbourhood, they promised. They showed us sketches and models, which we kept for the kids to play cars and Barbies with. We explained that we couldn't move because that gorgeous neighbourhood they wanted to build us all the way over in La Matanza didn't have room for a pond or for the Virgin, and even though the plans for the neighbourhood included a chapel, no one wants to live in a place called La Matanza, the butchery district, our Virgin included, and nor does she like being shut away inside, we explained. Father Julio was there and he told me that no, I didn't know anything about the Virgin, that they'd had her closed away in the churches for over a thousand years, ever since they'd started worshipping her too. Did you know that before then they didn't pay any attention at all to the Virgin, Quity? And that they'd never had any complaints from her, quite the opposite, and that the Virgin would appear to them every so often in some place and ask them to build her a church just like what happened at Luján, when in 1630 they had to leave a statue of her there. It's just like the one that's there in Luján now and the one on all the prayer cards from there and even on the police cars. Because, Quity, she's the patron saint of the police too. Sometimes I think the cops prayed to her more than we did the night before the massacre and that's why she didn't warn us, but she says that no, she had no idea, and she swears and swears and once she even cried and everything because I didn't believe her. I don't know. It must be true. The Virgin Mary can't lie, I don't think. Anyway, they'd been taking the Virgin of Luján somewhere in a cart and the cart stopped moving so they unloaded it and put everything but the Virgin in the road, but the cart still wouldn't budge so they unloaded the Virgin, who was just a little statue, and the cart moved, and they put her back on and the cart was stuck again. They did all this a thousand times and the same thing always happened, so they realised the Virgin felt like staying there and they took her to the house of nearby rancher. And she let them take her there.

They called her 'the rancher Virgin' and the 'poor man's mistress' too, which is like what they call ours, 'the Slum Virgin', except they didn't have slums back then. The ranchers kept the poor people like us crowded together, but they kept them in houses, Quity, not like us, kept next to the houses but outside them, crowded into the slum. Anyway, I was telling you, Old Manuel was little when the Virgin arrived and he fell in love with her and then the masters let him take care of her for his entire life. The Virgin likes us proles, Quity, and if we're transvestites she likes us doubly much.

Well, Father Julio told me this whole story and I told him I was going to ask the Virgin about the move, but that our pond had been her idea just like the cathedral at Luján, and that he'd admitted himself how stubborn the Virgin could be so what made him think she'd want to move now? Father Julio insisted, telling me it was for our own good and if we talked to the architects in La Matanza we'd surely find a way to fit in a pond. I didn't listen to him. I didn't understand. Now I think the whole thing about it being for our own good was a threat, but priests are almost always very diplomatic and you have to know them pretty well to understand when they're threatening you and when they're just giving you advice, although I'm not sure there's much difference between the two. I knew Father Julio pretty well, I even knew him in the biblical sense, I'd been between those sheets of his that he used to sprinkle with holy water, but that day I completely missed the threat. I reckoned that if it was important the Virgin would tell me. So we all left the meeting happy. Well, not everyone. I left happy, you were worried and the kids turned white when we told them about the new neighbourhood, but then someone turned up the music and we all forgot about it.

And anyway, bureaucracy in Argentina is so slow. Who would've thought the courts would move quickly for once, when we all had a load of friends in prison who'd been waiting four or five years just to face trial?

So when I heard the helicopters I thought they couldn't be for us and I didn't even step out of my shack to look up at them. I'd been cleaning and I didn't want to stop because otherwise I'd never get back to it, and the house was filthy. The kids did look up and they saw the sky fill with the dark blue of the police helicopters and before coming to tell me so I could pray to the Virgin they dug up the guns and all the weapons they'd had hidden ever since Saint Mary had come to the slum. Then they came to tell me.

Ernestito came over and when I asked why they'd waited so long he looked at me hard and told me that they didn't want me to dick around with pointless bullshit, that we were being attacked by land and sky and we had to defend ourselves and it was no time for a prayer circle, that I could pray as much as I wanted, that they'd talked to some of the pigs who'd ordered them to vacate the slum and that they'd said no and then the pigs ordered the women and children to evacuate, and the women said no fucking way, and then the pigs said they were going to come in and pull us all out anyway.

I grabbed Kevin by the hand and we went to the pond to pray to the Virgin. I prayed really hard, and I was pretty scared because I felt like our people had lost the faith and the Father, the Son and the Holy Spirit and even the Holy

Mother always make you pay for losing faith, Quity, so I prayed really hard and Kevin prayed too, but she didn't answer us. And when I heard the boom of the wall crumbling down it was the sound of demolition, my love, of bricks becoming rubble and squealing metal. Then came the sound of gunshots and everyone shouting and crying because they were wounded or because the pigs had shot one of their relatives or friends, and then I thought I really was *loca*. For the first time in my life I had a crisis of faith.

All of a sudden I felt like I was completely alone, talking to a chunk of cement while the world was falling down and nothing and no one besides us would protect us. So I grabbed Kevin again and went to the barricades the kids had built with the rubble and the sheet metal and the pieces of the geranium pots from the roofs. When I look back now it seems insane, we made barricades out of flower pots, my love, as if instead of a load of furious shantytowners we were a gaggle of demented hippies. At the barricade, I could feel the solidarity but there was still a horrific loneliness to everything, it was like when my mum died when I was a little boy, Quity. God and the Virgin had gone from the world, and only me and my little brothers and sisters and my beastly policeman of a dad were left. So I threw chunks of flowerpots, rubble and steel mesh at them and I also shot at them with an AK-47 the kids had handed me when they saw I was fighting too. Everyone knows I have excellent aim, Quity. My dad trained me when I was just a little boy and from the age of five I spent every Sunday shooting at a target in a field instead of going to mass.

I had Kevin by the hand the whole time, even when I had to aim he was curled against the bottom of the barricade, I swear to you, but then they shot Jonas in the head. He was right next to me, and I dropped everything, the gun and Kevin's hand, to try to stop the bleeding on Jonas's head, or what was left of it. It was just a second and I think that's when Kevin saw Pototo, that bald doll he loved so much, thrown in the mud. He ran out and I turned around right then, as if I'd sensed it, and I saw him cross the battlefield and I saw the bullet go into his head when he was just a few feet from the bald chef Pototo. He managed to stretch out his hand after the bullet was already inside him. He was dying, poor thing. I ran to him to hug him and so he wouldn't be alone, Quity, and I felt more alone than ever before, without the Virgin or God or any fucking thing, and I got hit in the head by a chunk of flowerpot and passed out, alone and mad and desperate and thinking that all there was left in the world was that very moment.

After I was knocked out by the flowerpot I don't know what happened. I only remember that two days later I was walking though Grand Bourg like a zombie with the Virgin in a plastic shopping bag, mumbling to myself. A trannie on her way home from work recognised me and took me to her shack and stayed up with me. We talked for hours by the fire she lit outside her door. It was very cold, and little by little I started remembering and I cried and cried and shouted and cursed the Virgin at the top of my lungs, saying the most horrible things I could think of. 'You cruel little backstabber' was the kindest thing I had to say. I ended up calling her much worse, I called her a 'fucking hypocrite cunt', 'fucking bitch son of a bitch traitor', 'pigeon-raped slut', 'slave to that almighty son of a bitch God'. I called her every name I could think of and nothing happened, no signs of life from the Virgin. She didn't turn up and I was convinced it had all been a hallucination, that there was no such thing as the Virgin or God or any fucking thing and all that was left was my body, and like you say, Quity, the bodies of our dead turning into worms and dirt and photosynthesis and shit and nothingness.

21. QUITY: 'BULLDOZERS AND BREAKERS'

Bulldozers and breakers,
they got a two-for-one
As they flattened out the slum
they laid the new foundation
for the rich bastards to have fun.

It wasn't like a tsunami or like an earthquake or like an avalanche. Or it was, but back then we lived like people who live in a place where they know these things might happen at any moment. In those places they fear the earthquake, try to run from the tsunami and build barricades for the avalanches, but they're taken by surprise whenever they come. They're never ready. The wounded or injured feel surprise before they feel the pain. Because you're never ready for a disaster. The ones who know it's coming avoid it. They get out of the way. What I'm trying to say is that no one is ever prepared for a bombing, for example, except for the ones that got away before it happened so it never happened to them. It's something that happened to someone else, to the place they used to live that's now just rubble and dead neighbours. Even the prisoner sentenced to death will be surprised by the bullet after hours watching the firing squad assemble and all the time hoping a tsunami will wipe out the soldiers, an earthquake will open up a crack and swallow them or an avalanche will leave them flattened. But these things never happen to the firing squad and if the prisoner's hands aren't chained he'll always use them to try and stop the bullet, cover his face like in the Goya painting or curl in on himself against the wall. I'm not psychic: we've been executing people for centuries and people always defend themselves the same way.

It's because it's is simply impossible to sit around waiting for death: life resists till the last moment. And when it stops resisting, it's because there's no life left. So there's no waiting, there's fighting and surprise until the end.

I don't know how much we fought and given that we lost I can't help but think it wasn't enough. It would only have been enough if we'd been an army but if we'd become an army we would've ceased to be what we were: a small happy crowd.

We resisted. We got Baltasar Postura to kill the Beast, the leader of lots of people who made our lives difficult. When the Beast's car crashed and burned on the motorway we thought we'd won and would be able to carry on in peace, since there was no one left to force the boys to go out and rob people or the girls to prostitute themselves. And in a way we were right: the Beast's boss wasn't interested in those types of business venture anymore. El Jefe had never been especially interested in them really. He wanted to build, to be the crest of the real estate tsunami. Somehow, and it's not so hard to guess how, he got the rights to that land. It can't have come cheap because the decision committee granted it unanimously. And he had Postura's blessing: ever since we'd got the carp, he hadn't been able to count on our boys to do his dirty work anyway. In exchange, El Jefe promised to build us a government housing complex on the last remaining land in La Matanza.

There were people who'd lived in El Poso for over

fifty years. They'd been there long enough to earn property rights, as any ranch family knows from the stories of their grandparents and great-grandparents about the origins of the family fortune. By which I mean, they fenced in the land and over the years that became a property line. I don't think it's hard to understand: there were five generations of slum dwellers who'd been born right there in that slum. Poor people begin to reproduce very young, so the littlest children in the shantytown were the fourth or even the fifth generation. And there was the pond, with the carp also predisposed to reproduction despite the already overcrowded conditions. And there was the Virgin, who was already the Slum Virgin and as much a member of the slum as her medium, my beloved Cleo.

We'd started to stockpile more weapons, but it wouldn't be enough. We never imagined anything so extreme. The gun dealers did, though; they followed the news and when they smelled the conflict brewing they turned up as if they'd always been there, as if they'd grown out of the mud, offering us everything down to mortars. I don't know what would've happened if we'd accepted them. El Jefe pulled his strings in the media and they started publishing articles about crimes committed by the kids from El Poso. These were in fact the crimes of other kids from nearby slums, but to the public all shabby shantytowners look the same and by the time the information had been corrected it was already too late, the idea that we were a pack of wolves had been solidified. Along with Cleo, I began to act as a spokesperson for El Poso. I was elected to the position because I was one of the few people in the slum who had a real command of the language.

We were pretty well-prepared, then, for anything that might happen, and we were even pretty well-armed. But we weren't an army; again, that would've meant ceasing to be

121

who we were, free and happy. We were aware of the threat, yes, but we never imagined the ferocity of the repression. They unleashed an entire army on us, I can only compare it to the Likud in Palestine. Machine guns, bulldozers and the order to advance at any cost. It cost us 183 lives. It cost them 47. But they advanced anyway. And here we are, in Miami, living like stars, after the period of paranoia locked in my loft in Buenos Aires and the period of grieving on the island in the delta of the River Plate. Wan has been in China and just returned to Argentina this year. Ginger and Rooster are in rehab. Helena's at the aquarium with her Klein and her chatty dolphins. The 183 dead are rotting or have already turned to dust in the Boulogne Cemetery. As for the rest, I haven't a clue.

22. QUITY: 'I WENT BACK HOME'

I went back home and I was alone in my loft with its controlled temperature, its light that shone with cleanliness and its well-stocked medicine cabinet. At first I felt relief. The twenty minutes it took the pills to turn to holy water under my tongue followed by the last moments of calm. Because that's when they started to appear, and they never went away: my ghosts are inconsolable. Nothing calms them down, not even quartering their executioners and offering up the parts or trying to save all the children who are still alive. Silence would not return to me even there among my old habits: I had my own bed, my cotton sheets and my feather pillow, and in the nightstand, my favourite gun. I put a knife under my pillow. Daniel brought me a machine gun that slept at my side like a girlfriend, I put grenades on top of my duvet and I surrounded the entire bed with landmines planted in the white carpet. I armed myself to the teeth: when I ground them, lightning shot out.

I locked myself away and didn't talk to anyone. All I did was watch the videos of the massacre. Daniel had got hold of them: the ones from the Secretariat of Intelligence, the ones from the German students, and the ones the kids from the slum had filmed on their phones. I watched them all a thousand times and a thousand times I couldn't believe what I'd seen on video and what I'd experienced first-hand.

Memory is fickle and it's been decades since videos could be considered reliable evidence, but what I didn't know then and would never find out was this: why hadn't they just killed us to begin with? Maybe to undermine us, to be able to tell everyone that a couple of trannie whores had gone insane. To reduce our credibility that way, by making the whole thing sound ridiculous. So they could say: 'If we'd wanted to kill them we could've poisoned their cement pond. But we didn't poison that dirty water filled with voracious whiskered multi-coloured carp.' And so they could follow their argument to the logical conclusion: 'No, of course we didn't shoot at anyone from the slum.' I was scared. I wanted to go back to that place that had first belonged to Jonas, to Cleo and little Kevin, and to the humble Virgin.

But Cleo showed up at my house, white from the shock and as mute as I was and then there was no going back. Her head was bandaged and she was wearing rags, broken shoes, carrying a cracked flowerpot with dirt and geraniums still growing out of it and the Virgin's head in a plastic shopping bag. She shut herself in the kitchen. She wasn't used to the dimensions of my flat. The three hundred square feet for a single inhabitant, with almost no walls, seemed inappropriate. 'Don't you get lonely here? This place is like a huge tent. What happened? Was it too expensive to add walls? You couldn't afford the bricks?' she asked me later, when she started talking again. She was lonely. She wasn't only having a crisis of faith, but the loft and the open view of the sky were also making her feel some kind of agoraphobia. She practically reduced her radius of movement to the kitchen, where she'd piled up everything she needed: the Virgin's head, a radio, a TV, her clothes, her wigs, hundreds of packets of crackers and boxes of pizza, her favourite food. I started going out a little. I needed to be alone and I was convinced that if they wanted to kill us they wouldn't be deterred by my building's doorman or any of my neighbours, so I used to go for walks, sometimes stopping for a coffee at the MALBA museum café. For some reason I couldn't explain, I felt safe there.

At home, Cleo and I would watch the news about the slum together. We even saw Cleopatra's funeral. That was the day she got her voice back. 'What fucking bastards, Quity! If they want to see me dead, I don't know why they don't just kill me and get it over with, instead of staging this soap opera. Do you think the Virgin's protecting me?' 'Don't be an idiot, Cleopatra, the Virgin doesn't exist,' I answered, having temporarily recovered my ability to speak too. But it left me again immediately. We hardly said anything for the rest of the day. We just watched her funeral procession, the service, the sobbing. Cleo was deeply moved. She cried as much as any of her mourners, like a little girl, she sobbed all day like a madwoman. There was a large crowd at the funeral home and the ceremony was extremely pompous. They somehow found, or maybe produced, a body the size of Cleo. Maybe it was a transvestite, maybe it was a large woman, it was hard to tell because the face was disfigured. 'Fervour Among the Masses at the Burial of the Controversial Sister Cleopatra', the headlines read. The service was given by the Bishop of San Isidro, a detail that touched Cleopatra greatly: 'Look at Father Julio, Quity, look at him, you see, I told you he wasn't so bad, you're such a sceptic you think that just because someone's a priest they must be a nasty piece of work. He's blessing my little boy and me.' 'Cleo, that bastard let them kill us and he abused you when you were thirteen years old.' 'Oh, Quity, he didn't send them to kill us and as far as the abuse goes, I wanted him as much as he wanted me. Besides, he taught me things about God and how to read properly and he sent me to night school and paid for my tits at seventeen. He loved me, and as for sleeping with me, everyone slept with me. And just look at the Virgin who got pregnant at fourteen by the Holy Spirit who was much older than Father Julio. Look how much he's aged, though. He looks like a grandfather. And those purple robes look fabulous on him.' 'Yeah, Cleo, you're right about that, your Father Julio looks like a sexy grandma.'

There were thousands of people at the Boulogne Cemetery. The bishop said that the church didn't acknowledge the sainthood of 'Carlos Guillermo Lobos, alias Cleopatra Lynch', but that even if she'd been a sinner she'd also been a good soul and that surely God with his infinite compassion would make room for her inside him. The priest really was convinced he was made in the image of his creator. Susana didn't miss the funeral, all in black and wearing a veil, showing off her newly sculpted cheekbones as she recounted the miracle that Cleopatra had performed on her when she'd been paralysed but then stood up and walked out of the slum one Sunday morning. No one talked about the poor people in the background; we never knew if it was out of fear or limited airtime. We just saw them throwing bouquet after bouquet of flowers they'd stolen or asked for at the gardens of the mansions that surrounded the slum and the cemetery.

They told us about it later in the letters they sent with the prayer cards showing the Slum Virgin and Cleo, Cleo with her bun like Evita's, her tailored skirt suit and fish in her hands. We saw online the shrines they built for her.

23. QUITY: 'IT WAS FROM INSIDE THE SORROW'

It was from inside the sorrow
that our love began to flow
Through broken hearts our passion surged
so she lifted up her skirt
and put it in me to the hilt.

One afternoon she started speaking again like normal. She recovered communication with the Heavenly Mother and after that she never shut up. As soon as I walked in, I saw the plastic shopping bag floating in an air current and Cleopatra kneeling in front of the head of the Virgin, which she'd set on top of my external hard drive. Cleo seemed ecstatic.

'I knew you wouldn't let me down.'

'. . . . .
. . . .
. . . .'

'It's true, Holy Mother, I thought you'd screwed us over. You sent us out alone on a suicide mission and you let them pump us full of bullets. They even killed little Kevin. I know they killed thou's son too but I don't give a shit. Yours came back to life, mine didn't.'

'. . . . .

. . . .,'

'And you're taking good care of him, Virgin dearest?'

'. . . . .,'

'I'm sorry, I'm sorry, but I can't stop crying, I'm sure he's better there with you but I miss him.'

'. . . . .,'

'Do you give him the ones he likes?'

'. . .'

'And what clothes does he wear up there in heaven?'

'. . . . .,'

'Yes, Holy Mother, hold me, forgive me for doubting you, hold me, I want to pray in your arms.'

'. . . . .,'

'Yes, like that, may God save you, Hail Mary, full of grace…'

I got furious. I gave her a slap that sent her backward onto the carpet and she came back to earth. 'You idiot,' I shouted at her, 'you fucked-up brainless idiot, what are you doing praying? You still believe that stupid crap about hearing voices from a shitty chunk of concrete?' She stood up and glared at me from her lovely height of six-foot-two: 'Quity, my love, come here,' she said and she picked me up and carried me to the bed, sat me on her lap and hugged me. She put on music, a Gilda track, very loud. She rocked me with my head between her enormous tits. And something broke inside me, something

128

opened up like the earth opens when the plates shift, something snapped, cracked like a dam under the pressure of a flood, something split in half, shattered like a window with a rock thrown through it, something collapsed like a bombed building, flaked away like the shell off a baby chick when it hatches from the egg.

I howled, unleashing an inarticulate, primal wail. Cleo stroked my head. My beloved has huge hands and with just one she held me and said, 'If you want to cry, go ahead and cry, love,' and she kissed me as I turned to water. I felt like I was coming undone, like I was being pulverised, like only a pile of dust would be left of me if I went on like that. I cried the tears Kevin couldn't over the bullet that left him dry and I was sure I was going to be left dry myself from so much crying. Cleo and I looked like Michelangelo's *Pietà*, with her as the mother and me as the child. She kissed me and touched me and I started kissing her. I started kissing her tits and I got them wet with my sobs and I got turned on and I wanted Cleo's dick like I'd never wanted any other dick before, or at least that's what it felt like at the time, and it seemed she wanted to give it to me too because she disassembled that unorthodox *Pietà* that we'd formed, spread my legs, stood up just a little and penetrated me with that huge dick of hers that seemed tailor-made for me. And I let her fuck me and I fucked her as she cried too. We were two desperate animals rubbing and smearing each other and feeling each other pulse like two people clinging to life.

'This is a miracle,' Cleo said when we'd finished and she ran to kiss the head of the Virgin. 'She's happy, she blesses our love and says it's about time I started a family,' my lover laughed. 'You see, my love, God does exist. It's like I died a little yesterday when they buried me and now I've come back to life as a different person. I've been resurrected as a lesbian, I think.'

My happiness didn't last long and I started crying again. Cleo hugged me again, again turning me into a blob held up by her body and she told me what had happened with the Virgin: 'I took her out of the bag to swear at her some more. Because she might be a saint and all that but she really screwed up and I told her so. She could've warned us, she could've done a miracle to save us, she could've at least sent some little angels to get Kevin out of there. She says she didn't know until it was already too late, that the Lord doesn't consult her or tell her anything about his mysterious ways, that they're mysterious for her too. But that she's going to teach the Holy Spirit a lesson. That shitty little pigeon, she said, he doesn't even disguise himself as a swan or a dragon for her, and he'll have to go down to hell to find someone to talk to because the Virgin doesn't want to see him again for a couple of centuries. She let me see Kevin. He looked adorable, all dressed in white with a nice ironed shirt and a pair of linen trousers, on a white beach too. The angels play with him all day: they line up in heaven like a squadron in a video game and Kevin pretends to shoot them with his little hand and they fall down like they're dead, almost down to earth, and Kevin laughs and laughs and for every angel that falls he earns a point and when he gets to a hundred points he wins the prize. A Happy Meal, with a delicious hamburger and strange superhero toys, saints, for example one was Saint George, another one was Gilda, another one was John Paul II, and Kevin plays with the toys and they give him sips of Coca-Cola and they stroke his head. The Virgin adopted him. Well, she didn't really have to adopt him because she was already Kevin's mother. She's everyone's mother, you know. And he has plenty of friends, little Yamila was there for example, happy because in heaven there are no stoplights and it doesn't rain and it's never cold, so she can play outside as much as she wants instead of having to spend all day looking at the stoplights and begging for change when the cars stop. The Virgin plays with the kids too, Gilda sings them songs and God answers all the silly questions they come up with and they let them eat all the crisps and biscuits they like in heaven and Walt Disney's soul, which isn't frozen like his body, makes movies for them and Doña Petrona, the nation's first celebrity chef, makes them crêpes with *dulce de leche*. Kevin's very happy because apparently God can answer his questions better than we ever could. I mean, after all, we hardly know why anything happens.' Cleo caressed me as she told me all about Kevin's heaven and I caressed her, and she had another erection, 'another miracle, thank you, my dearest Virgin,' she said, and we started to make love one more time.

24. QUITY: 'I DON'T REGRET OUR LOVE'

'I don't regret our love…' I was awoken by Cleo's singing and her morning aura, the smell of toast. It was the morning after our first night of love. Lit by the rays of sun that streamed through my windows, she appeared dressed like Gilda, with a black wig and a little red dress like the popular saint wore on the prayer cards. She danced and laughed. She finished her song with the words 'loving is a miracle and I loved you', set the tray on the bed and began to serve the *mate*. 'Good morning, Quity, my love,' she said. Through a mouthful of toast, she told me she'd never been into lesbianism before but that she adored me and we were going to be happy together forever. I said that yes, we'd be together forever, and that my panic had passed. At that point all I felt was fear and a desire to keep making love. And happiness, I felt happy that morning and in that happy mood we made our escape plan. I got the email I'd been waiting for from Dani. It was time to go. He and I had taken trips to the Paraná Delta together before. We had our kayaks in the same storage unit, which is where we always met to go rowing. We knew we'd be able to bribe the night watchmen to open up for us at 10 p.m. We had to leave before they got around to finishing Cleo off for real and we couldn't go by plane or train or bus. We wouldn't be able to leave from any station or airport if they were looking for her.

I don't think they can have been looking for her because we were perfectly fine at my loft. Those in power can be merciful too, when they feel like it. But we had to leave the country in any case and I knew of a route to Nueva Palmira in Uruguay. Slouched down in the kayak, with a hat, sunglasses, athletic clothes and a new haircut, and with the cockpit cover securely in place, Cleo would be able to pass unnoticed. The security guards usually indulged the more professional-looking kayakers. They'd think, like Cleopatra, '*mens sanos in cuerpores sanos*'.

Since I couldn't stop crying, Cleo tried to console me by telling me about Jonas in heaven: 'He's on a beautiful beach full of blonde girls and palm trees. A road runs along the shore and convertibles go past, driven by more blondes in sunglasses with scarves on their heads that blow in the breeze. They all look like Marilyn Monroe, like Susana and Evita, they're all gorgeous. He makes flying cars, learning from the best – Ferrari and Ecclestone. And at night he studies astrophysics. He's friends with Hawking, who's happy now: he has a body that works and he parties all the time. They listen to loud music played by the heavenly choruses. The saints and angels sing cumbia for Jonas. They wake him up every morning with that song he liked so much, you know the one, right? "Laura, your thong is showing," they sing to him in the mornings and he laughs and his eyes squint like when he was a little boy.'

We met Dani at the mouth of the Luján River, in front of our storage unit at ten at night. We'd booked a table and ordered spaghetti bolognese at the Fondeadero. We rowed up a few rivers, the Sarmiento, the San Antonio, the Dorado and the Arroyón. There was a full moon and we chatted quietly in the bright blue reflection on the water, in that silent, almost sacred space created by the rivers and trees. Dani wouldn't be coming with us. This was our goodbye.

We drank two bottles of wine that he'd been saving for a special occasion. And Cleo and I stayed on the island, and Dani went back.

25. QUITY: 'HE WHO HAS A HEAVEN'

He who has a heaven, should guard it and keep it safe: all the visitors, photos, articles and documentaries that splattered our images across the screens changed the way we lived in the slum. We'd tried to be discreet there, but it was a discretion tacitly understood by everyone: the people outside pretended there was nothing at all behind the walls, at the most they'd host a charity event every once in a while or they'd come and take photos or donate their old stuff. And the people inside the walls had always known that notoriety brought nothing but trouble. The press only paid attention to them when they were forced to evacuate their homes, or to cover a robbery, sometimes a murder or the odd cumbia song that made it to the charts. Nothing else.

Was that it? Had El Jefe been travelling in his helicopter when he saw a news story about us on his screen and a view of the slum under his feet? Years later, under Daniel's feet, he said something to that effect: he'd been going home, he saw the shantytown from above, he saw the roofs of the shacks blooming with geraniums, he saw the overcrowding, he saw the virgins and the saints, he saw the surrounding neighbourhood with the mansions of his business partners and he thought that the people in the slum didn't deserve to live so well, that his friends didn't deserve to suffer that proximity to them and that someone, like him, deserved to make a generous income off those lands. He would be the crest of the real estate wave. For us it was more like a tsunami. For powerful people like that, their desire is a force of nature, as real and undeniable as the law of gravity. Did he see himself as a hurricane that would blow all the sheet metal roofs out of the slum? Or as an avalanche, gaining force and growing larger as he pushed further forwards? Or did he see himself as an army? Or the law of natural selection, weeding out the weak to make room for the mansions of the strong? We'll never know.

Past a certain level a man must think of his wealth as a living thing he has to feed so it can grow and grow. Dani asked him and I asked him about it too but he couldn't or wouldn't or didn't know how to answer. Of course, when the tables were turned and he was the one listening to the questions, things weren't the same. He was tied to a chair, literally shitting and pissing himself with fear, his desire was no longer a force of nature and it couldn't even be called desire at that stage in the game. All the poor bastard had left was his survival instinct. He begged and begged like a fallen king: as miserable as anyone else, but slightly more prone to rage. I don't know why Dani took so long to kill him. He swore it wasn't sadism. He said he was hoping he'd tell us something, that he'd explain why. Why did you kill them, you piece of shit? He said he'd just ordered them to evacuate the area and that it was impossible to evacuate the area without killing anyone. He said if Daniel knew how to evict people without any casualties, he should come and work for him. He said he wasn't a bastard. He'd even got the government to agree to build a new housing project. And that hadn't been easy, he explained, no one gives up their land easily. Besides, he added, 'I didn't order anyone to shoot a kid, I didn't ask anyone to do that, I asked them to clear the area. My job is to come up with business opportunities.

I don't personally take the books to the accountants, update the computers, buy the cars, or clear the land to develop it. I'm the boss, I think about business, I do business with other bosses. I'm an important part of my company, but I'm not the entire company. I ordered them to clear the area, not to kill people. I'm not a murderer, I'm a businessman,' said El Jefe, the former businessman, the soon-to-be former person by that point.

I couldn't do anything. Ok, yes, I watched as Daniel killed him: he filmed it all as we video-chatted on our mobiles. I talked to El Jefe too. I needed to know. When I found out that Dani had kidnapped him, and that he'd had him gagged and tied to a chair for a few days in some filthy shack, there was no turning back. I honestly wanted to understand, Cleo. I knew he'd killed us to make money, but I refused to believe that Kevin had died for that cause. Because somewhere deep down I must believe in something too, I believe that life is somehow sacred and that slightly increasing a fortune which couldn't be used up even after two or three generations of Paris Hiltons isn't a good enough reason to kill.

I could almost understand it: nothing is sacred, and increasing a fortune, even slightly, justifies anything. It's not a matter of fortune, it's a matter of force. I understood that much. And I wasn't interested in killing him. I didn't hunt him down, I didn't kidnap him, I didn't shoot him. At that moment, when Dani called and showed me what he was doing and I participated in the interrogation by video conference, I thought the important thing was to send the message we've learned through all this: that force can only be opposed with equal force. And that avoiding revenge means condemning oneself to more suffering. Daniel finally got to do what he'd always wanted to do: for once, he was working on the good side of the arm of justice. He's not totally mad, he knew no one would miss the guy too much.

The government was sick of El Jefe's constant pressuring, his companies were all in other people's names and these people were also terrified by their boss's power so our Cuban friends here in Florida were able to buy them out at pretty reasonable prices, and where there'd once been a billionaire there were now several millionaires and even a trillionaire in his place. That's why Daniel was able to kill him. He shot him in the head, my love, I saw it clearly on the screen of my phone, and nothing happened: El Jefe just turned off like a machine. Daniel was still as bitter as ever but slightly less anxious. And I hung up and returned to your arms, to our bed, to our life that's protected by the cash from the cumbia opera and your fame. Fine, Cleo, we're protected by the Virgin too, if you say so. But she didn't do a great job protecting the slum, did she, if she was really one of us like you say? Oh, love, don't start again. The Virgin doesn't exist, Cleo. No, I don't know who the hell you talk to, my slum pacifist, my ballerina, my Joan of Arc. Just be quiet for a minute, okay, and take off these clothes for me. Yes, my love, just like that.

EPILOGUE

When I thought this book was ready to go to the printers, I left Cleo a copy so she could read it and give me her approval, just like she'd told me to. I decided not to include any chapters about the success of the cumbia opera *Slum Virgin* because that's something the world already knows about. It's all over the news, in magazines, it has a thousand fan sites on the internet and has even caused controversy between Cleo and the Pope... So why tell that story all over again? And I've just decided that from now on I'm going to devote myself to fiction anyway: you can't write your own biography with a wife who thinks she's a co-author, unless she's a writer too. Cleo asked me for a few days to read the book and decide what she thought. She left me a message in response. She called me by my real name in it, which is how I knew she was serious:

No, Catalina, dear, the story doesn't end there. It's not over at all: times of cataclysm and catastrophe are approaching and there are going to be new slums like El Poso all around the world. So it's far from over, that's not for you to decide. Also, the story of the Holy Virgin can't end with a murder and a shag. I won't allow it.

I know you think it's your book and that you can put whatever you want in it and end the story wherever you bloody well choose, but you're wrong: it's my book too and most of all it's the Virgin's book. I know what you'd say if you were here: that it's not your job to evangelise, and if the Virgin and I want our own book, we should write it ourselves. Well, my love, all the money you have is thanks to the evangelicals and the Holy Virgin. And writing's your job, that's your part in this story. Even though you did a bad job telling a fair few parts of it and you left a lot of things out. And now I don't have time to add it all into your book myself. Why didn't you write a chapter about the cumbia opera? Why don't you add in that every time I sing, fifty thousand people sing with me? And that five hundred thousand gringos have become followers of the Virgin since we debuted the opera? And that in Florida there are more statues of the Slum Virgin than American flags? That's not because of us, either, Quity: the fame and the dough come from the Virgin and through the Virgin and for the Virgin, and now the time has come to give it back to her. Make sure you put this all down just like I'm saying it, darling, because if not we're going to be in a lot of trouble. Beyond the trouble we'll be in when you hear this.

I'm sure you think it's ridiculous, but I'm going to repay the Virgin for our fame by preaching through the Caribbean. First I have to go to Cuba, Quity. Fidel won't be alive forever and not even the Virgin knows if he's going to heaven or hell, but even little boys and girls in China know the island's going to go to hell when he dies. And they're going to need the light of God and the Holy Virgin and I'm going to take her to them because she ordered me to.

When you hear what I'm going to say now you're going to get a bit more worried: I have to leave little Cleopatra with you. The Virgin says that times of cataclysm and catastrophe are approaching and 'it's better for the little girl to remain in her home'. Because the disasters aren't only going to happen in Cuba, my love, they're going to happen everywhere. There's already an economic crisis, and there's hunger, Quity. But what's coming is worse still: first the lights are going to go out. Mobile phones won't work. Nor will computers or the internet or the motors that pump the water to the buildings or anything. The war on Islam is going to leave us without petrol and the abandoned cars will block all the roads. There won't be any more shopping centres or TV or any form of communication besides ham radio, so you're going to have to learn to use one now, my love. There'll be no more antibiotics. No more frozen food. I don't know if you understand how big this disaster is going to be.

Here at the house there's a diesel generator, provisions, petrol, weapons, and canned food to last for about five years. You know better than me, you're the one who set up the bunker. I added the hens and the vegetable garden and Helena built the new pond in the middle of everything because canned food isn't a healthy diet and little Cleopatra has to grow strong. You thought I was just having an attack of nostalgia, that it was my way of being true to my roots, or something like that. But you were wrong: it has nothing to do with nostalgia. I built these high walls and crowned them with a Virgin, a statue of Saint George and millions of pieces of sharp broken glass because there's a catastrophe coming and I can't leave you two all alone and unprotected. I have to leave you for a while. And you have to stay here, taking care of little Cleopatra and Helena and her Klein, and the little Klein that's about to be born. Because our home will be saved, Quity, but that doesn't mean there won't be a battle.

There's going to be war across half the world, Catalina, listen to me. And everyone who lives and everyone who dies is going to need consolation in the years to come. The elderly will be dragging the coffins to the cemeteries, Quity, and they're going to have to pull the weight with ropes because, like I already told you, there won't be any petrol. Parents will have

143

to bury their kids, uncles and aunts will bury their nieces and nephews, and grandparents will bury their grandchildren. Everything will be back-to-front, the dead will be piled up everywhere because the old people will be too exhausted. And they're going to die too and I don't know who the hell's going to bury them. For all those who'll suffer, the old and the young and the middle-aged, I've built a cathedral to the Slum Virgin: anyone who wants to cry can cry at the feet of this altar and be consoled by the Mother of God herself, who provides the best consolation. This was the purpose of the fortune we made with the cumbia opera: to build the Virgin the church she deserves. It was all for her cathedral.

Yes, I know you're going to be angry, that's why I didn't tell you before, but the truth is I've already built the Virgin the shrine she deserves. The design was partly your idea too. It came to me when you gave me the eighteen-karat yellow-gold Rolex Pearlmaster with mother-of-pearl inlay encrusted with diamonds and precious stones, which I had to sell to build the altar to the Holy Mother. The Virgin wanted a portable cathedral, one that can go wherever I go. It's what she decreed. On the European tour last year, when you decided to stay at home and write because you said travelling bores you, I went to the Rolex offices in Switzerland and had them custom-make a portable monument to the Virgin. They loved the idea, darling. They liked my design, and they're all a bunch of Protestants and Jews that don't know anything about the Virgin, it's like she doesn't even exist for them.

They're the jewellers of 'eternal luxury', Quity, that's what it says on the side of the Rolex, so obviously they had to be the ones to build it. For her hair, we used 16,351 threads of twenty-two-karat white gold. The reason we didn't use twenty-four-karat wasn't to save money but because we had to add palladium and silver to make it brighter so the threads would shine like her hair does, blonde like a fire that doesn't burn,

144

like a Viking goddess. I don't know how to describe it: it's like it's lit up.

I gave her teeth, too. The best teeth you can imagine, my love, bluish white diamonds. I used sixty-four: the Holy Mother's smile throws off light like a flying saucer, like the summer sun, like a particle accelerator, it makes you feel like you've been cured of a fatal illness. And I put rubies on those thin lips of hers, fifty-five rubies. I gave her eyes too. Did I ever tell you about the Virgin's eyes? They're blue, but blue like the Mediterranean in Sicily, blue like the two giant sapphires I had brought over from Sri Lanka for her, Quity. The ancients, who you like so much, thought sapphires had the power of wisdom. They believed that when you were in a big fucking mess and you didn't know what to do the stone would solve everything for you. And that's what the Virgin's eyes are like: blue as wisdom.

The only thing Rolex didn't do was her skin. I designed her skin with Ivo Pitanguy, who might not be God but he's pretty close. Wait till you see the Virgin's skin and then you'll understand. We made it with sheets of chitosan, which is what they put on burn victims in the hospital. It's a kind of medical miracle, Quity. When you see the Virgin's face you'll understand. She has the skin of a baby.

The jewellers fixed everything else. What else is there, you're asking yourself. Quity, I couldn't make a gem like that and leave her unprotected. She's in a glass box that's more impenetrable than your bunker, dear: I bought it in Colombia, you know how down there the rich are always shooting each other, yes, I know, the poor too, but the rich shoot each other more there than in other countries so they've invented some amazing bullet-proof glass. They have, like, layers, of different thicknesses, for example the layer that's one centimetre thick can resist a .9-millimetre bullet shot from 4.57 metres away and with a bullet speed of 394 metres per second, and it can take three impacts like that. The box I had made is thirty centimetres thick, my love. You do the maths: they'll use up all their bullets before they even crack this glass. And it's electrified, too. It only stops giving off electricity if I touch it with my fingerprints, and my skin has to be between thirty-six and thirty-eight degrees, my love: I can't open it if I'm dead or I have a fever. And it films, Quity, it's like a black box with images, it records everything that happens in a circle of 343 metres all around with a definition of seven megapixels. And it has the latest technology in loudspeakers with an AMP of 4x120, which is as powerful as the speakers we use when we do the stadium shows. The computer we put in is programmed on a loop, it plays church music all day, like cumbia and the Ave María and other songs about the Virgin. It recites the Hail Mary too, Quity. It understands the orders I give it and then it sings, plays music, prays or does nothing.

It has its own generator too, that I had made with dynamos and pedals like a bicycle. I have to pedal ten Hail Marys per day, which is the minimum we should be praying in times of crisis anyway. And I can get some exercise in the meantime too, my love. When I get back I'll be as fabulously fit as ever.

I'm leaving you this radio that's synchronised with mine. And don't worry, planes are still flying at the moment and for when they stop I've already talked to a group of boatmen who can get me back across to Miami when it's time for me to come back to be with you, my love, and with our daughter. In the meantime, I don't how long it'll be but the Virgin said it won't be too long. I'm going to record messages like a diary of everything that happens. Because this has to be written down, and you're going to have to write it, my love.

I'm going to Cuba to find her. I don't know if I'm heart-broken or if I have a grenade where my heart used to be. I also have no idea if I'm going to be facing a divorce or the

Apocalypse. I don't understand what happened. Maybe it's not so easy to abandon one's origins, and in Cleo's culture of origin moving away with all the money and leaving the child at home with the woman is something any male can do without damaging his honour or good name. But I don't think Cleo is precisely male. She loves her daughter and truly believes in the Virgin. So it must be true that she turned that sad chunk of cement into an outrageously expensive and outlandish eyesore, and that she's in Havana now trying to organise a mega-concert to convert the Cubans to the faith of the Slum Virgin. If I weren't so furious with her, the process of rewriting the cumbia opera as a text worthy of the Revolution would be thrilling. But all that's left in our bank accounts is a measly 300,000 dollars. And we had ten million. And my beloved moved away without even warning me first. She took off with all the cash and left me alone with the child, like I'm some kind of, I don't know what, her little homemaker! Of course, I sent her a response:

Carlos Guillermo Cleopatra, you're right, this doesn't end here. I'm coming to find you, we're going to sell that hunk of metal and precious stones you call a cathedral and you're going to go back to praying to the chunk of cement you saved from the slum, which has done us pretty well until now. I'm sure your Virgin will serve you just as well without any gold or diamonds. With the money we get back I'm going to pay for you to have some psychiatric treatment. If you don't come back willingly, I'm going to sue you for theft. I'm going to ask for you to be extradited. And you're going to be sent back to Argentina in handcuffs and not even Fidel, dead or alive, nor all of your fan clubs combined, will be able to stop it. I'll see you in Havana, love of my life.

CHARCO PRESS

Director/Editor: Carolina Orloff
Director: Samuel McDowell

charcopress.com

Slum Virgin was published on
80gsm Munken Premium Cream paper.

The text was designed using
Bembo 11 and ITC Galliard Pro.

Printed in February 2020 by TJ International
Padstow, Cornwall, PL28 8RW using responsibly sourced paper
and environmentally-friendly adhesive.

MIX
Paper from
responsible sources
FSC
www.fsc.org
FSC® C013056